DANUBE STATIONS

To Philip and Diane,
with good wishes

Howall Wilson

May 16, 2007

DANUBE STATIONS

J.D. Mallinson

To order additional copies of this book, contact:
Xlibris Corporation
1-888-795-4274
www.Xlibris.com
Orders@Xlibris.com
29659

For my son John and son-in-law Robert

PART ONE

DOWNSTREAM

CHAPTER ONE

Major Peter Lang was a prominent figure in MI5, with a reputation for relentless pursuit of suspects in the world of intrigue centred on foreign embassies and trade missions in London. His main concerns were activities, particularly in the area of personal life, which might involve any kind of risk, no matter how slight, to the security of the state. His successes, in the dozen or so years he had been in the job, had earned him a formidable reputation, and as he made his way northwards across Hyde Park on the morning of July 15th, he was confident of being able to add significantly to it. Rarely had Major Lang felt so confident of himself.

The closeness of the weather made him glad to be away from the confines of his office and in the comparative coolness of the park, amid the tourists, the strollers, the military bands. As he strolled unhurriedly beneath the trees he spared one eye for the relaxed activity around him, while keeping the other firmly fixed on the figure ahead of him, a well-built man who walked with the distinctive gait of an American serviceman in the direction of Marble Arch. Lang was tailing him on this particular morning, as he had done on the same day and at approximately the same hour for the past two weeks, from the moment the figure left the American Embassy in Grosvenor Square until he reached his destination. He was a junior member of the Military Attaché's staff, going by the name of Lieutenant Robert E. Cramer, USAF.

On this morning, as on the previous occasions Lang had followed him, Cramer walked the length of Hyde Park from Knightsbridge to Marble Arch, then crossed the Bayswater Road and continued north along Edgware Road, as far as Wessex Square, where he would enter the premises of *The Antiquarian*, a bookshop specialising in early editions of European manuscripts. He would browse awhile among the musty shelves before collecting at the counter a weekly newsletter and bibliophile magazine. On regaining the street, the airman was observed on several occasions to remove a brown envelope from inside the magazine and place it inside his uniform. He would then continue north along Edgware Road, enter the underground and board the Circle Line Westbound, alighting south of Hyde Park, a short distance from Grosvenor Square. One of Lang's staff, Malcolm Evans, took over at the Edgware Underground and tailed him back to the American Embassy.

Lang's interest in Cramer had begun as the result of a tip-off from the Military Attaché, Colonel James Manderson, about suspected leaks of information from inside his own department. They had singled out Cramer initially because he was a third generation East European immigrant, the family name having been changed from Kruminsky at the time of his grandfather's naturalisation in the USA. He was also the newest, and the least tried, member of Manderson's staff; and it was Lang's guess that *The Antiquarian* could be some sort of repository for classified information—it provided perfect cover—and that one of its employees, if not the owner himself, was Cramer's accomplice.

As Cramer entered the bookshop on the morning of July 15th, Lang signalled Evans, who appeared to be examining the display of briar pipes in a tobacconist's window opposite. When the American eventually emerged they challenged him, confident of catching him red-handed.

"Lieutenant Robert E. Cramer?"

The airman checked his stride, a wide boyish grin masking his surprise.

"Peter Lang, MI5," the major curtly explained. "I must ask you to accompany us to headquarters, where you may be able to help us with our enquiries."

"Hey, what is this?" Cramer immediately countered, feeling sudden unease at the vaguely familiar name. "An arrest or something?"

"Merely routine, Lieutenant," Lang said, disarmingly. "My car is waiting over there."

"And if I refuse to help you with your enquiries?"

"That is your privilege, Lieutenant," Lang conceded. "But if you do that we may have to lodge a request with the Home Office for withdrawal of your visa. I am sure you would find that very inconvenient."

Cramer's gaze faltered and he glanced away, for once uncertain of himself, wondering how much they knew, how much they were guessing. What a stroke of luck that there had been nothing for him that day at the bookshop. The police could raid it right there and then, but they would find nothing in the least incriminating. He had taken nothing there himself for the last few days, and in fact did so only at infrequent intervals when specifically asked to do so. It had been a mistake, however, to visit *The Antiquarian* so regularly; so much he recognised as the grim faces of the two security men confronted him.

"Very well, gentlemen," he said, at length. "If that's the way you want it. Lieutenant Robert E. Cramer at your service."

Evans signalled the car parked at the next corner. It nosed gently forward and pulled up silently at the kerb. A rear door opened and the three men clambered inside. Then it sped off in the direction of Whitehall, Cramer sandwiched between the two security men. The seriousness of the situation then seemed to dawn on him for the first time, and he began to view the prospect of possible deportation with considerable misgiving. It would mar the whole progress of his operation, just when it was at its most sensitive. He had, however, been anticipating official interest for some time, following a tip-off from inside the Embassy, by a girl who worked in Security; and he had one significant card to play.

Lang and Evans maintained a stony silence; it was part of the game of nerves, now that the man was in their charge. When they reached headquarters, Lang sent Evans for a stenographer, ushering Cramer into his private office.

"Take a seat, Lieutenant," he said, drawing up a chair facing his desk. "Cigarette?"

The American pulled out his own pack, flicked one into his palm and lit it with a flourish. Inhaling deeply, he crossed one leg over the other, admiring the crease in his uniform trousers, and waited to hear what the Major had to say. Evans's sudden disappearance made him feel slightly nervous.

Lang glanced first at his watch, then at Cramer.

"Just about now, Lieutenant," he said, icily, "your accomplice at *The Antiquaian*, Beverly Maddern, will have been taken into custody for infringements under the Official Secrets Act. You might as well come clean and tell us your end of the story: it will go easier on you in the long run." Having trotted out his stock speech, he leant back in his chair to await its effect.

Cramer's complexion changed from natural bronze to dark pink. He continued smoking his cigarette, but said nothing. He's bluffing, he told himself, again thinking how lucky he had been. If he had been caught red-handed that would be something else. Lang had blundered.

"There is other evidence, Lieutenant," the Major continued. "In the testimony of a colleague of yours at the Embassy. He saw you examining files to which, with your present rank, you do not have official access. What do you say to that?"

The airman glanced back coldly at his interrogator; apparently he knew more than he had at first suspected. It was Davidson he was referring to, and the incident mentioned had taken place two months ago: it could not mean that much, or he would have heard about it sooner.

"Then there are your visits to the bookshop at Wessex Square. The same hour each week, Lieutenant, regular as clockwork?"

"I enjoy good books."

Lang smiled, leaning forward with hands clasped on the desk.

"So do I, Lieutenant," he said. "In fact I bought a rare first edition myself three days ago at an antiquarian booksellers in Pimlico, a mere stone's throw from your Embassy."

Cramer smiled. In a way he admired Lang; he had a nice sense of irony. And if he really had arrested Beverley—it was possible, since she had not been at the shop that morning—that would place the entire operation under scrutiny. Lang was bluffing, he decided. And Colonel Manderson would be very reluctant to suspect one of his own staff. He had that kind of loyalty.

"You still have nothing to say, Lieutenant?" Lang pressed, with increasing impatience. And where was that confounded Evans with the stenographer?

Cramer said nothing. He merely crossed and uncrossed his legs, took out another cigarette and lit it, his eye fixed on some point behind his interrogator's head, a calendar picture of the harbour at Brindisi.

"I want names, Lieutenant," Lang then said, pointedly. "I want the names of everyone in the syndicate, which I have good reason to believe has ramifications far beyond the City of Westminster."

Cramer was impressed. Lang had evidently done his homework, and he would give a lot to learn exactly how much MI5 knew, or merely suspected. But there was a world of difference in this game between suspecting and knowing: one had to be caught red-handed. A great many people carrying out highly sensitive jobs in every capital in the free world would not bear scrutiny if their affairs were examined too closely.

"There are no names," Cramer said, through a cloud of blue-grey smoke. "I told you, I am a book collector."

"Who is S?" According to Lang's informants, he must be someone fairly high up in the Whitehall establishment; someone who was protecting Cramer, while making use of his services.

"We know all about S," he went on. "But we want you to tell us what *you* know."

Cramer smiled. "I have no idea what you are talking about," he replied. "There is no such person as S. You must have dreamt it."

"Oh, S exists all right," Lang persisted, reaching for the inter-com and wondering what had detained Evans.

Cramer listened impassively to the major's curt instructions and found himself wishing the MI5 man would show just a spark of humanity; pull out a cigar, perhaps, or a decanter of whisky. He sat in such puritanical judgement over his fellow men that for several moments Cramer hesitated to prick the bubble of self-importance and conceit. No one in MI5, he felt sure, knew of certain key facts in Peter Lang's less-recent history.

"Does the name Martin Ahlers mean anything to you?" Cramer eventually asked, taking the opportunity of Evans's continued absence.

The heavy palm of the MI5 man hovered in mid-air over the inter-com, which he was again about to bellow into. It seemed to hover for several seconds before it locked tensely with his other hand on the pink desk blotter. His expression changed from one of imperious smile to one of acute surprise and embarrassment.

"I never heard the name before," he said, tersely.

"I have it figured that you have," the airman persisted. "You knew him intimately as Oberleutenant Martin Ahlers, in the Rhineland in 1945, for several months prior to the Allied invasion."

"I know of no one by the name of Ahlers," the major insisted.

"In that case I shall have to refresh your memory for you," the American said, unbuttoning his tunic pocket and extracting a photograph from it, which he held up just out of the other's grasp. It was a picture of Martin Ahlers among a group of German officers at a reunion in Mainz. In the centre of the group were the unmistakable, if younger, features of Peter Lang. "Are you *sure* you did not know him, Herr Breitman?" Cramer asked, with a quizzical smile.

Lang coloured deeply and said very quietly: "How did you come across this photograph?"

Cramer smiled. "Ahlers is in London."

"And he gave it to you?"

Cramer nodded.

"A turn-up for the book, eh Major?" he said, with a hollow, resounding laugh. "Who would expect to find an ex-Nazi practically running British Security?"

Lang rose from his desk and crossed to the window, from where through the slatted blinds he could see the tourist launches on the Thames. He bit his lip until it bled, clenched his fist in mute, impotent rage at the treachery of Ahlers, the cunning of Cramer. The former had evidently been bought; in fact, he must have come forward with the information, volunteered it for financial gain. Everything of course was true. He had taken the identity of a fallen British Officer at the end of the war, escaped to Canada and subsequently returned to England with a flawless record and background. No one but Ahlers, who had helped him, could connect him with his original past. Until now!

He turned from the window and said, icily:

"I suppose you want money?"

"What would it be worth, Major? Your career ruined at its peak. Public disgrace. Prosecution even, for identity theft at the very least. If the press got even the slightest inkling . . ."

Lang paced the room, like a caged animal. The atmosphere of the interview had completely changed, from one of interrogation to a contest of equals, each deadly at his own game. He sat down again and watched the airman keenly, with a grudging respect that nearly equalled his distaste.

"Very well," he exclaimed, as if he still had the upper hand. Evans was now visible through the glass panel in the office door, the police stenographer at his side. "Wait," he bellowed, in answer to the knock.

"Well, Major?"

"If you agree to hand over the photograph, I shall be prepared to suspend enquiries for a period of three months. That will give you time to sort things out for yourself and put in for a transfer."

Cramer slowly shook his head, a smile of amusement playing about his cynical lips.

"No dice," he replied. "For one thing there is more than one photograph. The other one, a copy of this, is not in my possession." He glanced at the wall calendar again, checking the date, and said: "Soon it will be lodged in a very secure quarter, kind of permanent insurance for me, if you like, to be used whenever and however I think fit. As for my presence in London, that also is to be as permanent as I or my superiors see fit. The one guarantees the other so to speak. Do you understand my meaning, Major?"

Lang's face turned ashen, as he realised the full implications of what Cramer had done. The airman looked on, with the satisfaction of completing a particularly expert piece of work.

"You bastard," he muttered, with a distinct hiss. "You had this up your sleeve all the time."

"So far as we understand each other, Major," the lieutenant said. "That is my main concern."

Even then Lang was not entirely sure the man was not bluffing. But he was too damned plausible to be taken lightly; and the consequences, particularly for his wife and family, were too ghastly to contemplate. That Ahlers of all people should have done this to him! To what depths of depravity had his former compatriot sunk, that he would betray a former fellow officer?

"You expect me to commit treason?" he enquired, in the same hissing voice. "To betray the values of the service after half a lifetime of public work? There is a limit, you know, to what a man, specially a trained officer, will do to save his skin."

"Even if that means trial and imprisonment?"

"Get out!" Lang snarled, contemptuously. "You have my assurances that the matter of the bookshop will be dropped."

"That is all I wanted to hear, Major," Cramer said, with a look of triumph as he strode towards the door. "And one more thing, Major. There is no such person as S. You do understand that clearly, don't you?"

"Fully," replied the major, tersely.

"Then good day, gentlemen," he called as Evans held the door open. "And happy hunting!"

"What the . . . ?" Evans stammered.

"As you said yourself, Evans," Lang explained, "we moved too hastily. Nothing changed hands at Wessex Square. We have no reason to detain the Lieutenant. Have a drink on me." He dismissed the stenographer and pulled out a drawer of his desk that doubled as cocktail cabinet. There was a grim smile on his face as he spoke, not unlike that of a man being granted his last privilege.

"You look as if you've seen a ghost, sir," Evans said, still trying to make sense of this completely uncharacteristic about-face of his chief. "Are you sure you're all right?"

"Put me a call through to Zurich," Lang said, uncapping the whisky bottle. "At once!"

CHAPTER TWO

When Chief Inspector Harrington bade goodbye to George Mason at the ticket barrier of the morning boat-train, it was with firm instructions for a complete rest from his normal course of duties. Mason was not even to help old ladies find missing handbags. In his view, his subordinate had been heavily taxed in recent months after a succession of demanding cases culminating in a plot to discredit a leading member of the government. Mason, for his part, was only too relieved to be quitting London for a while, in exchange for a fortnight's cruise on the Danube. It was sensitive terrain, as far as his department was concerned, but there had been a temporary lull in international activity. Inspector Mason envisaged nothing more demanding than fourteen days of pleasant cruising on calm inland waters, having no taste for the open sea. It would also afford him the opportunity of visiting several European capitals which, in the normal course of events, would have been virtually impossible. He felt gratified that the Chief Inspector had taken the trouble to come down to see him off; it reassured him as to his chief's interest and concern, aspects of Harrington's character which, in the normal course of professional life, did not rise so readily to the surface.

As the boat-train pulled slowly out of Victoria, Harrington waving frantically at the barrier, Mason withdrew his head into the compartment, watched the disappearing tenements of Brixton and Clapham South, and settled down with a carton cup of British Rail coffee to read his Bannerman guide. It was a paperback reprint of a famous series compiled just before the outbreak of the Second World War; and although political events had superseded it in several important respects, it still remained the best general guide for the tourist interested only in a first-hand account of the more classical tourist sights; and Mason for one was not interested in the precise location of the Belgrade Hall of Justice, or in the Budapest Museum of Atheism, both of them examples of recent post-war construction. He would stick to Bannerman throughout, trust to the old German's thoroughness and sense of proportion; for Bannerman had one advantage over the other guides he had examined, despite its grey hairs: it included between one set of covers all the major cities through which the Danube flowed, from Vienna to the Black Sea. That, for George Mason, entirely justified its inflated price for a paperback, even with plate photographs, at three pounds fifty.

He was much intrigued by the riverboat. The *Orsova*, a vessel of shallow draught, rode gently at anchor on the rising swell of the Danube, dwarfed by the sheer size of the river and by the imperial proportions of everything else in the Austrian capital. For Vienna was built in the grand style, with interminably long boulevards which made the journey from hotel to quayside, accomplished on foot, far more arduous than he had anticipated. Tourists were boarding in a steady trickle off the quay, having emerged from the Customs House. He noticed a suitcase marked M. J. Woolcot, Surbiton, Surrey; watched its owner, a dark-haired, slim and conventionally dressed young man grip it in his right hand and mount the gangway. He felt reassured, for he had not really anticipated fellow travelers from England. It would facilitate social contact.

The boat proved much larger than it had at first appeared, most of its bulk remaining hidden below the quay. A young Rumanian dressed neatly in cream shirt and dark-green trousers, the livery of the ship, took his luggage and conducted him to the lower deck, where he had booked one of the lesser cabins. There was a distinct smell of the river, the dankness rising up to greet him from the vicinity of the wash basin in the unwholesome darkness. He gazed hopefully at the single port-hole too far above his head, and thought: had I been on Harrington's salary, I could have run to a cabin on A-Deck, with a view of the blasted river. He accepted the key, tested the bed with his full weight and found it soft and comfortable. Removing his shoes, he lay full-stretch and rested his pavement-weary legs.

When he arrived in the main bar for the Captain's Welcome, the First Officer, resplendent in white braided uniform, was addressing the ship's passengers through the Intourist guide, while the waiters, trays borne aloft, plied them generously with free drinks. Amid the thick knot of Germans, retired workers from the Ruhr and the Saar, their bank-rolls in dependable Deutschmarks bulging at the hip, he espied M. J. Woolcot and elbowed slowly closer. He stopped when he saw the young Britisher surrounded by a group of fellow nationals of approximately the same age as himself, each of them displaying the badge of Globus Tours. There was something about the tour mentality that to Mason, the lone agent, was distinctly foreign. One was apt to become too organised, to have it decided in advance what was worth seeing and what was not; more or less on the lines of a Sunday school outing.

Woolcot, however, had already sensed his presence, and drew him firmly within the fold, introducing him in turn to Clare Dyment, Gayle Sumner and Oliver Markham, who was a geography teacher from Slough. The two girls, in common with Mike Woolcot, were civil servants.

After separating to unpack in their cabins and individually explore the boat, they met up again on the foredeck just before dinner; all except Gayle Sumner, who had decided to take a rest. They watched fascinated as the *Orsova* cut a shallow draught in mid-stream, holding its course equidistant from either bank—the guide explained that for want of rain the river level was very low— on its way through lower Austria and across the border with Czechoslovakia. There, in the gathering dusk, which came earlier in that latitude than in England, they passed a large town on the left embankment, a garden city with lawned terraces descending to the water's edge; but also with a certain air of modernity that spoke of post-war renewal.

"Bratislava," Oliver Markham declared, with his air of spokesman for the group, but George Mason was more interested in the posture adopted by Clare Dyment, and whether the distance of approximately half a foot which she maintained between herself and Mike Woolcot, both of them from the Foreign Office, was accidental or intentional. There was no doubt in his mind as to the intentions of the young diplomat. He regarded the secretary as booked for the trip. Taking stock of his fellow passengers, George Mason had decided that, amid the superannuated German tourists and the English party, there was simply no one else available. He resolved to give gentlemanly chase, since the girl seemed to expect it of him. She said:

"Have you been in Eastern Europe before, Mr. Mason?" He thought the formality a bit unnecessary.

He shook his head. "I was in Zurich once," he said. "And before that in Brussels. I am not what you might call a seasoned traveller."

"In that case the Danube will be all the more exciting for you," Clare said. "There is nothing quite like the sensation of discovery, to shake off the accumulated dust."

"It all seems well documented to me," the pedantic Oliver said. "People have been this way before, you know."

"Yes, but for us it is an entirely new experience. We must discover it all afresh for ourselves. Take the romantic instead of the pedestrian view."

George Mason wondered if the young woman wasn't being a little too romantic; whether the Captain's Welcome, combined with the fresh breeze coming off the water, hadn't gone to her head. In any case, it was an approach he preferred to that of the geography master from Slough, who seemed bent on reducing everything to navigational statistics.

"It is your privilege, Miss Dyment," he remarked, "to discover everything afresh, to see the world through an explorer's eyes."

The girl seemed to detach herself a significant few inches more from her professional companion, who in any case was absorbed in taking snapshots of Bratislava with his Instamatic camera. Leaning towards the detective, she said:

"That makes you sound very mature, Mr. Mason. Yet I shouldn't have thought that . . ."

Mason shrugged off the veiled enquiry. Old as one feels," he said, evasively. Just then, in the keen evening breeze and the beams of the setting sun, a dull-red globe dipping into the river behind them, he too felt a sudden surge of romance, the excitement of travel.

"Life begins at forty or so they say," Oliver Markham observed, in his own defence, since he was the eldest of the group. By that time one ought to have sorted out exactly what one wants from life, and pursue it to the hilt. No more side-tracks; no more red herrings."

Mike Woolcot had mentally rejoined them, sharpening his observation now that the mysterious Mr. Mason was the subject of conversation; as if he already sensed in him a rival for the attentions of the girl.

"By the way, George," he began. "What do *you* do back home? You haven't told us yet."

Mason drew out of the pocket of his sports shirt a neatly rolled cigar and lit it pensively while rehearsing his reply. There seemed little real harm in disclosing his actual profession; yet his instincts fought against it. It might set a barrier between him and them. They might come to feel that they were being watched even when they were not—although the idea seemed far-fetched in surroundings such as these. Worst of all, it would undermine his sense of vacation, the very thing Harrington had warned him against.

"Go on, George," Clare urged, as everyone looked his way. "Do tell us!"

"Perhaps he doesn't work and is ashamed to admit it," said Oliver, who was beginning to sound more and more like the schoolmaster he was. "Or perhaps he won the pools."

George Mason laughed, despite himself. What an idiot that chap was, and whatever did his pupils make of him?

"Let us say that I am in regular employment," he confessed, after a while, "and leave it at that."

"I am surprised we did not put in at Bratislava," Woolcot said, changing the subject. "It's a fair-sized town from the look of it. And the *Orsova* makes no other call in Czechoslovakia."

"That might be on account of the political situation there," Clare thoughtfully remarked. "It's a far more sensitive area than, say, Yugoslavia, or Hungary."

"A good point," Mason said, determined to support Clare Dyment in everything she said, so long as it was not too outrageous or fanciful. "These Intourist people know what they are about, what to show to visitors, what to leave out."

"That sounds like an expert view, George," Woolcot said, wondering if he had not met Mason somewhere before. The trouble was that in his line of work one met a constant stream of people. And he had difficulty in placing a face.

"Just a thought," the detective quipped, discounting the other's earnestness. "Simpligessverk."

"I can see our Mr. Mason has a certain wry sense of humour," Clare Dyment suggested. "But you are doubtless right in what you say. I don't suppose they will show us much of what the real Hungary, or Yugoslavia, or Rumania, is about. It might not suit their image of themselves."

"Since we shall be free to roam around at will whenever we disembark," Oliver said, "I think that is an unfair accusation. They can't hide a whole city from a handful of tourists. And why should they wish to do so?"

"Oliver has a point," Mike put in. "We shall have to take things as we find them."

"Except that, with luncheon here, tea somewhere else, in between the guided tours, there won't be much time to look around."

"Speaking of which," Clare said, as the Intourist guide, a well-built and conventionally attractive Hungarian named Magda, hove into view from the lower deck and briskly approached them, with a look somewhere between curiosity and contempt, as if they were the victims of capitalist exploitation.

"Everything is . . . satisfactory?" she enquired, with just a hint of uncertainty, thinking perhaps of the cabins on B-Deck, which were susceptible to light flooding.

The quartet nodded, equally wary, wondering if she hadn't something else in mind.

"We arrive in Budapest at midday tomorrow," she announced. "There will be a guided tour of the city which I personally shall conduct, lunch at the Zigeunerhof, with wine and music."

"Sounds fine by me," Oliver Markham said at once. "Put me down for it by all means."

"In the afternoon there will be a tour of Castle Hill, the old city, and the fortifications, followed by a visit to a leading philatelist's. Hungarian stamps prove popular as presents."

"Interested?" Mike asked Clare, in a bid to secure her company for the afternoon. He seemed already to have divined a certain independent streak in George Mason, the lone wolf, which did not accord with the guided tour. He was right. George Mason vigorously declined. Clare then appeared undecided herself, but was persuaded by the Zigeunerhof, noted for its gypsy music. Perhaps she also reasoned that the voyage was barely begun. There would be time no doubt, during the long hours on deck, to cultivate personal acquaintances.

"Just the three of you," Magda said, disappointed that it was not all of them. "And the second lady member of your party? Will she also come?"

"Miss Sumner went to lie down before dinner," Oliver explained. "She was tired by the journey out. I should think you can put her name down too."

"Very well," said the guide, emphatically, with a stern glance at the recalcitrant Mason, who merely shrugged.

"Collect your meal voucher from the purser when we dock. You can exchange them in any of the state hotel restaurants in Budapest."

"Oh?" said Mason, nonchalantly. "And which ones are they?"

"All of them," replied Magda, who remained speaking with them for several moments, about this and that, really quite intrigued at discovering English tourists on board, in what had hitherto largely been the preserve of Germans, Austrians, Swiss, the odd French. Her manner was synthetically friendly, Mason thought, edging to the rail to watch the slowly changing, fascinating landscapes of southern Czechoslovakia. One would never read her true thoughts or feelings; she composed it that way.

"You promised to loan me that book," Oliver reminded Mike Woolcot, as the dinner bell sounded. *"Bannerman's Guide."*

"Hang on, I'll fetch it straight away."

CHAPTER THREE

B y the time they had dressed and breakfasted the following
morning, the *Orsova* had already taken them well within
the borders of Hungary, with its landscapes of darker greens, rolling
farmland, timbered farmhouses and a backcloth of coniferous forest.
The river had filled out considerably, but not enough to prevent
them gaining firm impressions of either bank, details of which were
carefully noted by Oliver Markham in the unofficial log he was
keeping of the voyage. Before midday there loomed before them
the splendid vista of Budapest, divided neatly into two halves,
Buda on the right, Pest on the left, with an impressive fortress
commanding, from a rocky outcrop, the water approaches to the
city. The view was so riveting that everyone on board, including
the Intourist guide who had seen it so many times before, gathered
as far forward as they could to gain the maximum advantage from
the slow, stately progress of the *Orsova* right into the heart of the
city, where it berthed at the Elizabeth Quay amid the morning
bustle of the Hungarian capital.

The coach for the guided tour had already drawn up alongside,
attracting the attention of the passers-by and the city youths on
the quayside steps, equipped with improvised fishing rods. Magda
Semyonova commenced herding her charges off the boat as soon
as the gangplank was lowered, checking off their names against a
list in her hand. The coach driver promptly roused himself from
his mid-morning nap; which suggested to Mason, watching from
the rail, that he had been waiting for some time. His impression of
socialist countries was that anyone employed in an official capacity
did quite a lot of waiting about; orders were so impersonal and

bureaucratic, to his way of thinking, that it took time to give them effect. The Germans, serious in contrast with their late-night carousing in the forward bar, filed on ahead, followed by members of the English party. Gayle Sumner, fully refreshed and more eager than any of them, led them on, with a parting glance at the solitary Mason.

"Are you sure you won't come along?" she seemed to say, with a girlish enthusiasm for group travel. "You will be lonely by yourself."

The detective shook his head and smiled back, pleased that the girl, uncertain at first, had accepted him as a friend. The geography master followed her on, followed by Mike Woolcot and his secretary, who also glanced back.

Mason waved them off, but he was waving mainly at Clare Dyment, until the coach disappeared from sight beyond the Elizabeth Bridge. It was one of several Danube bridges, stately constructions that had replaced those destroyed in the Nazi retreat, presenting the casual tourist with an embarrassing choice of direction, between the two halves of the city. Instinct directed his steps away at right angles from the Danube, into the heart of the old city of Pest, detailed in his Bannerman guide. There were few enough people on the streets, which was surprising for a city of that size. That might be explained by the hour of day, not quite the hour of lunch, when the inhabitants were probably hard at work fulfilling whatever economic plan had been devised for them.

He was impressed at the number of churches, conceived in an age of faith and executed in the ornate baroque style that seemed common to Catholic churches in Central Europe; open churches, with dim, musty, candle-lit interiors, empty of worshippers. Yet they remained accessible; one could just as easily enter as pass them by. There was no overt persecution of creeds inimical to the official materialism. Perhaps that was achieved in subtler ways, by discouragement, scorn, loss of privilege. He strolled in and out of them, past equally deserted cafés, shops and stores, unaware that the streets would come alive after normal working hours, when the shops would be at their busiest and remain open until late at night. Life was organised differently than in Western countries, and he began to regret the independence of spirit that had led him to eschew the official tour, the company of Clare and the rest.

He must find something on his own, to compete with the Ziegeunerhof and its much-vaunted gypsy atmosphere; some single experience that would justify his independence of spirit, something more memorable than a litany of visited churches, cathedrals, museums and monuments—those petrified embodiments of a nation's spirit; some savour of its authentic living soul; something with which to impress Clare Dyment after dinner in the lounge bar. But all there was was this rather dispirited-looking collection of buildings, their inhabitants invisible behind impenetrable walls; the cafés empty; the churches deserted. At one time it must have been vastly different, an imperial city throbbing to the music of gypsy bands, to the zither and the violin; a city of colour, of vitality, of joy. Now all the joy seemed drained out of it. But was that merely a personal impression, conveyed by a quiet hour of the day?

The Vlad Hotel flanked a large square with well-laid gardens, opposite the Cathedral of St. Stephen, and at right angles to the Ministry of Culture and Sport. It was listed in his dated Bannerman as a premier eating establishment, once patronised by visiting royalty—not royalty of the British kind, he considered, but of the more prolific, less durable, Central European variety. Of palatial proportions, the restaurant was like some vast palm court, with tropical plants in large earthenware jars; with frock-coated waiters and a string orchestra that played vaguely familiar melodies. It must be equally as good, he thought, as anything the redoubtable Miss Semyonova had to offer. And why not try the beef stroganoff? It was the only dish on the menu that he knew, amid the Tokanys, the Lesco, and the Pogacsa.

He did not at first notice the woman sitting at the next table, separated from his own by a thriving rubber plant of huge proportions. She was peering inquisitively at him through elaborate spectacles. No longer a young woman, but towards middle-age, with the sort of grooming and dress that suggested a successful career woman.

"Can I be of any assistance to you?" she enquired, politely. "I am sure you must be English."

The sound of his own language, tinged with dulcit, but unpronounced American tones, startled him. He had tacitly assumed that upon leaving the tour party at the boat, he had immersed himself in a totally foreign environment. Apparently, it had been a false assumption.

"I was having trouble with the menu," he confessed. "But I've already decided on the stroganoff. If you would care to join me?" He made a quick calculation of the amount of his exchange *forints*, and decided that his budget could stand it, since his own meal was covered by the *Orsova* vouchers. But the woman had already eaten.

"You could offer me a coffee," she said, with a coaxing smile, transplanting herself with alacrity to his side of the non-flowering shrub. "It's not often one meets an English tourist out here, cut loose from the organised tours."

"You aren't a tourist?" he remarked in some surprise, wondering how she could be so certain that he was. Behind the deep lenses, her eyes were difficult to read.

"Heavens, no!" she cried. "What would an American tourist be doing in the Vlad Hotel, without a guide, an interpreter and an official party? We're not so independent as that."

"Then you must work here Miss . . . ?" he said, beckoning the waiter. "A job at the Embassy, perhaps?" As soon as he said that, he realised that it did not fit.

"Mrs. Aveling," she explained. "I am a widow, and I do work in Budapest, among other places. A kind of roving commission, one might say." But she seemed disinclined to add more.

A saleswoman of some sort, he imagined. A representative of an American company, possibly in cosmetics. She looked the type, with her carefully-applied make-up. It was not that important, and he was not going to pry.

"You came off the *Orsova*, didn't you?" she said, amused at his surprise. "I merely guessed, because it is due through here today. Comes the same way once every two weeks, during the main season."

"I was enjoying some solitary sight-seeing," he confessed, with a rueful smile. "Haven't much time for guided tours."

Mrs. Aveling smiled as if she understood; as if she was a kindred spirit.

"Have you visited the Cathedral yet?" she asked.

He nodded.

"Then you should also take in Castle Hill—on the other side of the river across Elizabeth Bridge; the Karolyi Palace; the

University Chapel and, if you're interested in art, the National Gallery on Roosevelt Square."

"You're beginning to sound like a guided tour," Mason exclaimed humorously. "But I am grateful for the advice."

The American fell silent for a while, watching the waiter perform the elaborate ritual of serving the meal, and noting the Englishman's reaction to it. She seemed pleased that he found it to his liking.

"May I glance at this?" she asked. "Haven't read a Bannerman's guide for years. They're almost unobtainable now."

"Help yourself," Mason said, generously. "This one's a paperback."

For some reason he had placed the book face upwards on the table, between the small carafe of wine and the cruet. She nudged it gently across the table cloth, so as not to disturb anything, but also as if it were fragile. "It is still the best guide," she remarked. "Although partially out of date."

"I almost bought Nagel's instead," he confessed, "but the salesman persuaded me otherwise."

Mrs. Aveling nodded, as if in agreement. Mason returned to his meal, which was expertly prepared, if a little rich for his palate. He was not at all anticipating the next move. The waiter crossed to his table and presented a salver bearing a slip of paper. He took it and read the hastily scribbled note, his eyes opening wide in incredulity. Mrs. Aveling gave a puzzled frown.

"A note from someone," he said. "Seems I'm wanted on the telephone."

"They asked for you by name?"

He nodded curtly, and rose uncertainly, thinking there might be trouble at the boat. But that was impossible. Nobody knew of his direction that morning. Or did they? He thought for some reason of the secret police, then of Harrington's injunction at all cost to avoid involvements.

"I'll be back in just a minute," he said. "Don't go away. I want to hear more about the Karolyi Palace."

The telephone booths were just outside the restaurant double doors, inside the main foyer. He went straight to the one indicated by the waiter, fishing in his jacket pocket for a *forint* piece to tip him.

"Mason," he said, speaking expectantly into the receiver. There was no reply. Mason looked around him in a slight panic, saw nothing unusual and repeated his name. Then he heard something, not a word but a heavy breathing sound, before the phone clicked and the line went dead. What the hell . . . ? he thought. A practical joker. But who knew him? Who could know him, in the whole of Budapest? And what was their game?

He returned irritably to his table, surprised to find that Mrs. Aveling was no longer there. He was not unduly worried. She might simply have gone to the Ladies Room. He was more concerned about the phone call, and thinking about it spoiled his enjoyment of the meal. He pushed it aside three-quarters eaten, and ordered black coffee.

By the time he had drunk the coffee and smoked a cigarette, the American woman had still not returned. It was then that he noticed his guidebook was missing. Something clicked instantly in his brain: it was Mrs. Aveling who had arranged the bogus phone call! He flung the meal voucher down on the table, dashed past the dumbfounded waiter and out into Engels Square.

There were several alleys leading off. He chose one, Zrinyi Street, and followed its tortuous, cobbled way until it issued in Vorosmarthy Square. He sank down, out of breath, on a simple wooden bench by the entrance to the metro station, realising that chase was useless. Mrs. Aveling and his Bannerman guide had simultaneously disappeared, probably for good. What on earth could she want with his guide book, he asked himself, wondering if he should not report her to the American Embassy? But that would waste the remainder of his time; he had only a couple of hours to see anything of Budapest.

There were more surprises in store for George Mason when he reached the *Orsova*, still feeling bitter at the loss of his guide book, and wondering if it would be possible to lodge an official complaint. When he had washed off the grime of the Budapest streets and gone up to the dining room for a dinner of baked river fish, he discovered Clare Dyment in a state of acute anxiety over the absence of Mike Woolcot, whose private cabin on B-deck she had already checked twice since returning from the conducted tour. The boat was by this time in mid-stream, half an hour out of Budapest and bound for Belgrade, with the bare eastern plains on the one hand, and the lush, fertile valleys of Transdanubia on the other. There was no question of stopping the boat, or of a return to port, which was her first adamant suggestion.

"He must be *somewhere* on board," Mason remonstrated, in an attempt to soothe her feelings, being careful not to reveal his own misgivings. "Did you try the bar lounge? I know he likes a drink before dinner and he may have missed the bell."

"Oliver and I between us have combed the whole boat," Clare complained, glancing at the geography master for confirmation. "It's not as if it's an ocean liner. There isn't much room to get lost."

"We think," Markham said, gravely, "that Mike did not rejoin the cruise in Budapest."

"Impossible!" declared the detective. "You must have been with him the whole of the afternoon."

"Most of the afternoon," Gayle Sumner said. "The last time I saw him was on Castle Hill. He was buying picture postcards."

"That was the last stop before we returned," Oliver explained. "He may simply have missed the bus."

"And you haven't done anything about this?" Mason asked, his anxiety growing at every minute.

"We've been trying to contact Magda," Gayle explained. "But her office is shut and she does not take dinner until later. I think she may be in conference with the Captain."

"So old Mike missed the bus," Mason said, beginning to see the humorous side of things. "You must have been close to him, Clare. Did he board the bus at Castle Hill, or didn't he?"

Woolcot's secretary flushed. "Well," she said. "I was almost sure he did. But I fail to see now how he can. I mean he couldn't have."

"You didn't ride back with him?"

"I was one of the last on. I remember talking with a German woman—she's over there on the far table—and we had to scramble aboard at the last moment."

"Didn't Magda check the numbers?"

"It all happened in such a rush," Gayle explained. "We were afraid of delaying the boat. The guide mentioned something about currents. I don't think she checked the numbers."

"I saw him enter the Kossuth Tower," Oliver explained. "While I walked on ahead to the Fishermen's Bastion. What he did subsequently I have no idea. I also assumed he boarded the bus, but none of us saw him do so."

The baked river fish arrived, but none of them ate with much appetite. Clare Dyment, who had considered treating everyone to a bottle of Hungarian wine, decided to postpone it, pending news of Woolcot. Mason could sense that they all now looked to him, as the most resourceful member of the group, to do whatever was possible. While he ate, he mused silently on the best course to adopt, feeling how ironical Harrington's parting injunction had been. What else could he do in such a circumstance than begin to play the detective?

"It has been a day of strange happenings," he remarked, mysteriously, when the meal was well-launched.

"What do you mean by that, George?" Clare asked, nervously. He liked the way she spoke his name, with a soft, north-country lilt. At a guess she might be from his part of the world, but years of living in the capital had modified her accent. Just now it suited him to play the role of her protector, in the baffling absence of her colleague.

"I mean that my Bannerman was stolen—or perhaps it was merely borrowed without my consent—by an American woman in the restaurant of the Hotel Vlad."

"What American woman?" Clare and Gayle exclaimed in unison.

Mason outlined to them his movements through the old part of Pest, how he had eaten at the Hotel Vlad and met an American, whom he took to be a saleswoman in cosmetics. Then he described the bogus telephone call in the hotel foyer, and the curious result.

"It sounds kind of strange," Gayle said. "I mean, as if the two events—Mike's disappearance and the theft of your book—were somehow connected."

George Mason froze that line of reasoning at once. It was too close to the bone of professional detective work; and he had no brief, neither from Harrington nor from anybody else, to start poking his nose into everyone's little problems and coming up with sinister solutions.

"They are just two strange circumstances, in the heart of an East European city, Miss Sumner," he said, rather stiffly. "Don't let your imagination work overtime."

"All the same," Clare Dyment said. "It is rather a strange coincidence, isn't it?" Seeing the look of animosity on Mason's face, however, she changed emphasis. "Was the book valuable, Mr. Mason?"

"In financial terms, no," he replied, curtly. "In fact it was a paperback edition of the very book you have there with you. I bought it on Smith's bookstall at Victoria Station."

"Just an ordinary paperback, like any other?"

"Exactly like the next. Not a first edition, not a special edition. Nothing in the least remarkable about it. I can only imagine that Mrs. Aveling . . ."

"At least you know her name," Oliver quickly prompted.

". . . that Mrs. Aveling, if that is her real name," Mason continued, "picked it up by mistake and placed it in her shoulder bag, before leaving the hotel."

"I'll go ahead and order a bottle of wine, after all," Clare stated, emphatically. "I think we all deserve a drink."

"Instead," said Mason generously, "let me offer you a brandy with the coffee. It'll do us more good."

The trio eagerly accepted.

"All this speculation and mutual commiseration isn't really helping poor old Mike," Gayle Sumner objected. "Shouldn't we have told someone before now. Lodged a complaint?"

"What good would it do, in the middle of the Danube River, several miles south of Budapest?" Mason enquired. "I expect he simply missed the bus, back there at the Castle. He'll know what to do all right. Isn't he a professional diplomat? He'll simply contact the British Embassy or Legation, or whatever it is they have here. And they'll probably arrange transport down to Belgrade, where the ship calls next. On the other hand, they might radio the captain to put in an unscheduled stop inside Hungary."

The commonsense and unemotional approach appeared to steady even the nervous Miss Dyment, who had remained anxious about Woolcot throughout most of the meal. The group now relaxed to the tune of imported brandy and strong coffee, watching the river slip effortlessly by through the port-side windows. The sun began to dip into the water behind them, somewhere over Vienna, their point of departure from the West. None of them at this point seriously entertained sinister forebodings; the voyage, and their hopes for it, were too young for that. They began to view Mike Woolcot's misadventure in a more urbane and slightly amusing vein, now that their stomachs were well filled and the euphoria of the evening cruise descended on them.

"All the same," Oliver Markham eventually decided, "I think we should at least report him missing and have the captain radio ashore to the British Embassy. It would be the correct formal procedure."

"Of course, Oliver, of course," Mason agreed. "I'll go and see to it without delay."

The two girls joined Mason and Oliver later in the lounge. Dinner had filled out most of the evening, and after dusk there was little to interest them beyond the shadows of trees and buildings, and occasionally of people, dimly glimpsed on the nearer shore. They returned to the bar and ordered drinks, competing with the far more boisterous Germans for the attentions of the hard-pressed waiter. Gayle suggested a game of bridge to occupy the time, but it seemed inevitable after a few hands that they would return to the subject of Mike Woolcot.

"Magda was most concerned," Mason observed, "when we tackled her about it. Couldn't for the life of her imagine how he had been unaccounted for at the Castle. Must have counted somebody else twice, she said."

"You're not going to swallow that, are you?" Oliver challenged.

"It is simply not good enough," Clare Dyment said, sternly. "Mike is probably lost and extremely distressed, not least at the thought of missing part of his cruise."

"Magda may know more than she cares to admit," Oliver said, ominously.

"Now take it easy," Mason placated. "There's no sense in reading too much into this. The captain radioed ashore to the Budapest Port Authority, and they have promised to contact the city police and the British Embassy. There was nothing more that they could do. He was very angry at the Intourist guide. Said it has never happened before."

"Did he mention anything about putting in an unscheduled stop lower down, like you suggested?" Clare asked.

Mason shook his head. "It's a question of the currents," he explained. "The *Orsova* has to keep right on course for Belgrade, where the harbour is deep enough. He explained that water levels were low following last year's drought. As it is there is a possibility of being grounded."

"That explains the dipping sticks going out all evening," Gayle said. "I watched them myself before dinner. They must be testing the depth all along."

"That's a fine state of affairs," Clare Dyment said. "Not that they would mention such a possibility in the brochure. And they certainly charge enough."

Mason was intrigued at the last remark. On a secretary's wages, a Danube cruise might well be an expensive holiday, as it was on a policeman's salary. Had she made the sacrifice to accompany Mike Woolcot? It began to look that way.

"Don't worry about water levels," the knowledgeable Oliver reassured them. "This vessel hardly displaces any; it'll get through all right. In another day or so we'll be waving to ocean liners."

They took comfort in his reassurance and settled into the game of cards, much as they might have done in the bar of an English pub; except that they were surrounded by Germans on the Danube River, with another five days' sailing before they reached its outlet, so vast and intriguing and exciting did it seem. Fully as romantic, too, as legend portrayed it; yet now with a strong undercurrent of mystery, inspired by the fate of Mike Woolcot.

"Don't all look at once," Clare said, ominously, "but I sense trouble."

One of the German-speaking party had detached himself from the rest and commenced walking unsteadily towards them, grasping the chair backs on the way whenever the ship rolled slightly with the current.

"I am sure he was with Mike at the Kossuth Tower," she explained in a hoarse whisper, as if that fact implicated him in her colleague's disappearance. "I don't know why I didn't mention it before, but they were together for most of the afternoon, since we ate lunch at the Zigeunerhof. He seemed to fasten onto Mike from then on."

"Interesting," Mason remarked. "Then why didn't he also miss the bus back?"

"Permit me to introduce myself," the German began, standing over them and speaking in rather formal, textbook English. He was elderly, with a wisp of white beard flowing into a bow tie. "Anton Ziegler, Cabin Twelve."

The group half rose and acknowledged him cautiously, afraid that he might intrude on their game of cards.

"I was hoping to meet again Herr Woolcot, of Your Majesty's Foreign Service, but I have not seen him all evening. Could you tell me if he has remained in his cabin? Perhaps he has a slight indisposition, and that would be a pity so early in the voyage. This afternoon he seemed so . . ."

"You were with him this afternoon?" Mason asked, at once.

"Why, yes, of course," Herr Ziegler replied, rather surprised. "He has in his possession a book in which I was much interested. A first edition of *Bannerman's Guide*, which would be quite valuable as a collector's item. It is the plates, you understand, that make it so rare. They were not included in later editions."

"You are interested in old books, Herr Ziegler?" Clare Dyment asked, feeling her suspicions ebb.

"Perhaps you are not aware," Ziegler continued, "but as I explained to our dear Herr Woolcot, I am a dealer in secondhand and antiquarian books, prints and maps. I have my business in Zurich, on the Niederdorf."

"Were you with Mr. Woolcot when he entered the Kossuth Tower?" Mason asked, sharply.

"Er, no. As a matter of fact I was not," he replied, with a strange smile. "I went instead to visit the Bartok Archives which are housed close by. You see, a large part of my professional interest lies in music manuscripts of various kinds. Not that I wished to buy any of the Bartok material—it is far too priceless a national treasure ever to be offered for sale on the open market—but merely to establish if I could the authenticity of an early Bartok signature which was offered to me in Zurich last spring. By a political refugee from Prague, as a point of interest. He escaped in '68, but kept the manuscript hidden all this time."

Mason felt that he was straying from the point, perhaps consciously throwing up a smokescreen about manuscripts to divert them from the real issue. But in that case, why had he come over at all? Was it maybe to check that Woolcot had not returned? And this confounded guidebook again! It had an international reputation, in England, America, Switzerland . . .

"You did not know that Herr—I mean Mike—Woolcot failed to return to the *Orsova*? That he was somehow delayed, or lost track of time in the Kossuth Tower, and failed to board the bus back to the dock?"

The Swiss drew back in alarm, raising himself to his full height of six feet, with the absurd goatee beard twitching nervously.

"You do not say so, Herr . . . ?"

"Mason," the detective said, appraising him carefully.

"But this is most alarming," the Swiss said. "Surely you will by now have contacted the police and the civil authorities in Budapest? They would be most concerned to think that something, that someone . . ."

"The authorities have been notified," Mason confirmed. "But since you spent at least part of the afternoon with him perhaps you may have noticed something out of the ordinary; something suspicious in his manner that may help account for his sudden disappearance?"

"Why, nothing at all," Herr Ziegler said, after only a moment's reflection. "I am sure I would have noticed if there had been. We spent an enjoyable lunch together, and after that we went our separate ways. He seemed quite cheerful and relaxed."

He went away muttering to himself, while the group applauded Mason's efforts.

"You were great," Clare said, in enthusiastic admiration. "One might almost have thought you were a professional . . ."

Mason did not let her say it. As Harrington had warned him, this was to be a holiday from start to finish, and even if Mike Woolcot had met with some misfortune on Castle Hill, then he was going to leave the matter entirely in the hands of the Hungarian State Police and the British Embassy in Budapest.

"If Herr Ziegler merely wanted to examine the book," Oliver explained, "he could borrow it from me. Mike lent it to me last night, and I forgot to return it this morning. He then produced it from his jacket pocket, where it caused an obvious bulge. Markham was the type of Englishman who invariably wore a jacket, even on sultry river evenings like this.

"May I borrow it, instead?" George Mason asked, on sudden inspiration, now that a certain train of thought, hinging largely on guidebooks had begun inside his professional brain. Curious, he thought, how at least three copies of the same book, although in different editions, had appeared on the same cruise. Which one really interests them? he wondered. And who are *they*, the faceless people? And what has that old goat Ziegler got to do with it all?

"Sure," Oliver said, genially. "Be my guest."

CHAPTER FOUR

They had travelled far during the night. Already, by the time they had breakfasted, changed for the deck, and gone up to take advantage of the morning sun, the *Orsova* was sailing past Mohacs, the last settlement on the Hungarian side of the border. The scenery had changed little, and they were not expecting it to do so until, as Magda had explained earlier, they reached the foothills of the Transylvanian Alps and the deep gorges south of Belgrade. The same fertile plains stretched beyond the riverside villages as far as the eye could see, with Lake Balaton vaguely imagined on the distant horizon. The sun shone unabated from a cloudless sky. By midday the heat, were it not for the cooling effect of the water and the breeze made by the ship's passage, would have been unbearable. The two girls, Clare and Gayle, had changed into bikinis, the Germans into shorts; while Oliver Markham and George Mason, low on tropical kit, sported slacks and open shirts.

The geography master was reminiscing for the benefit of anyone within earshot on the course of the Turkish wars, which had reached a critical point in the region of Mohacs. Herr Ziegler was performing callisthenics with a group of Swiss, as ever it seemed to Mason keeping within observation and speaking distance of the English party. Mason himself sat in a deckchair, in one hand a bottle of Hungarian lager, in the other the original edition of Bannerman's guide.

"I thought your subject was geography," he quipped, having let Markham's discourse distract him from his book.

The other man turned. Slow of thought, and of riposte, he was equally slow to take offence.

"Humanities, actually," he explained. "It includes history."

Mason relapsed into silence, ignoring the drone of the victorious campaign of Sullimein II. It must have happened centuries ago; what was the interest now? More recent events, perhaps, would be worth recounting; but there were few enough signs of the Second World War, or of the later Russian occupation. Everything lapsed into oblivion, given time; or perhaps it was only seared on the people's memory, the racial memory that gave rise to heroes, legends and folklore.

Now that he had the book in his possession, he intended to make full use of it in preparation for his shore excursion in Belgrade. He was conscious as he perused it, even from a distance of some thirty yards across the deck, of Herr Ziegler's continuing interest. Was it worth that much, he wondered, examining the fine tooling, the handsome binding and the expensive plates that subsequent editions did not run to. A collector's item in the literature of travel? He sipped his beer, glad that the bar had served it chilled, lit one of the duty-free cigars he had been careful to store in on his way through Holland. Or was it more than that? Was there some connection between this book, so evidently prized by the Swiss, and its pale paperback counterpart abandoned as a hostage to fortune in the restaurant of the Hotel Vlad in Budapest? There was no reason at all for him to imagine that there was, apart from the workings of his suspicious mind. Yet the notion persisted; the more so perhaps since the copy he now held so provocatively in his grasp was really the private property of Mr. Michael Woolcot of her Majesty's Foreign Service now, for reasons known only to himself, landlocked in the Hungarian capital. That prompted the further question: was there a connection between this book and Woolcot's misadventure? The sternly paternal features of Chief Inspector Harrington intervened between question and answer, defying him to take up the challenge. He let the book drop gently to the deck, half expecting the eager Swiss to abandon his exercises and make a dash for it. But Ziegler merely followed its progress with his eyes, noted its final resting place and continued with his exercises.

Mason shrugged—perhaps Ziegler wasn't so interested after all—and fell to wondering what they would have for dinner. Mealtimes were a highlight of the cruise and he would be glad when they reached Belgrade. He would be glad too when Clare Dyment re-opened her eyes to the world at large, after spending most of the morning acquiring the perfect sun-tan. His eyes travelled the length of her long, slim, pink-tinted limbs, round the mature curve of her hips, the hollow of her stomach, the taut bosom and the slender, ivory neck, fringed with hair of a golden brown. It had lightened several shades since leaving Vienna, owing to the effect of the sun. She would be interested in him, he felt, were it not for the nagging presence—or rather absence—of Mike Woolcot. And he could appreciate her point of view. An up-and-coming member of the diplomatic corps; someone with whom she would maintain at least a close working relationship the moment they returned to London. London, with its traffic fumes! It seemed light-years away.

It was mid-afternoon by the time they reached Belgrade, heralded by a commuter express racing alongside them on the left embankment, its windows jammed with friendly Yugoslavs, dressed uniformly in workmanlike denims and waving frantically after them as their train forged ahead. The ship's passengers waved back, in a spontaneous gesture of good will and also perhaps because, after almost a full day afloat, the sight of a train full of people was an event in itself. The ship's horn sounded, as much to forewarn Belgrade of its proximity as in reply to the train's whistle. Even before the *Orsova* had docked, Mason was down at the Intourist Office on B-deck to check with Magda Semyonova if there had been any news of Woolcot.

"The captain radioed ashore this morning," she explained, obviously worried and much embarrassed by the incident. "And again just after lunch. He was extremely concerned, and he holds me responsible. I may even lose my job."

The fate of the Intourist guide, to whom he had taken an uncharacteristic dislike, did not concern him in the least.

"Is Mr. Woolcot to rejoin the cruise, now that we have reached Belgrade?" he asked, impatiently.

"There has been no official communication regarding Mr. Woolcot," the girl explained. "But there is no cause for alarm. It is doubtful that he contacted the city police, since he does not speak Hungarian. Unknown to the authorities, he may have gone straight to his Embassy, who could have arranged private transport down to Belgrade. It would be legitimate, since he has tourist visas to cross the border. Wait and see what happens when we dock. If he is not there, the captain has promised me that he will go in person to the Belgrade authorities, to have them look into the matter."

"If he is not there . . ." Mason mused, half-aloud. That was a possibility he had not seriously entertained. But the girl's eyes remained inscrutable, trained as she was in dealing with truculent Westerners. She merely shrugged, in a rather casual bureaucratic manner, as if she had done everything expected of her. Mason decided to make future representations direct to the captain; the more go-betweens there were, the more tenuous the lines of communication. And the captain had courageously made the matter his personal concern.

"Any luck?" Clare asked anxiously, the moment he returned to the sun deck. She had earlier accepted his offer of dinner that evening in Belgrade at a rendezvous to be determined by Bannerman. She would steal away from the organised tour as soon as it had completed its initial circuit of the city, a part of the official programme she was determined not to miss.

"No official communication of any kind," he said, despondently.

The girl looked disappointed, and at the same time incredulous. It simply could not be true, her eyes seemed to say.

"That may only mean that he did not contact the local police in Budapest, on the grounds that he did not speak the language," Mason hastened to explain, passing on Magda's one grain of comfort. "The British Embassy may have taken full charge of the matter."

"You mean they will have arranged for his transit through Hungary and into Yugoslavia?"

"Exactly."

"Will you invite him to dinner, too, if he is there?" There was a certain girlish plea in her voice that he could not resist, much as he disliked the idea.

"In the circumstances," he said laughingly, "what else could I do?"

"You are a sport, George Mason," she said, squeezing his arm. "I love you for it."

The detective smiled ruefully to himself, that the word should come so lightly to her lips.

If they had expected to see Mike Woolcot waiting jubilantly at the quay they were disappointed. Even George Mason was disappointed, even though it meant that he would be able to enjoy Clare's company unchaperoned. Magda Semyonova made an ostentatious double check of the passengers boarding the coach, as if determined not to lose anybody this time. Clare exchanged anxious glances with Mason, who went to have a word with the guide to see if she could not spur the captain into action. It had been agreed between them that, failing Woolcot's reappearance, Mason should forego the tour and head straight for the British Embassy. They would meet later back at the boat before going off together to dinner. He noticed that Clare too had a copy of *Bannerman's Guide*, a hardback not dissimilar in appearance to Mike Woolcot's, at the moment safely locked away in Mason's cabin.

As the coach moved off after the short delay on Woolcot's account, Mason was amused to watch Herr Ziegler take up the vacant place beside the girl; the place he himself would have occupied in more normal circumstances. His intention seemed to be to buy up all outstanding copies of the guide book, for his first noticeable action was to borrow the book from Clare, and settle back with it into the plush upholstered seat. What's in a book, Mason thought, that it should command such sustained interest? Especially when the sights would be more than adequately explained *viva voce* by the voluble, perhaps too voluble, Intourist guide? On impulse he retraced his steps to the anchored *Orsova*, to retrieve the first edition from his cabin locker. He would probably need it, to locate the British Embassy; but his immediate motive was caution.

Belgrade struck him as somehow livelier than Budapest; its people gayer, less careworn, as they strode with lilting confidence along the broad, tree-lined boulevards. Perhaps it was merely the hour of the day. Turned four o'clock, most of them would have finished work and were now doing their day's shopping in the teeming shops and stores; queueing for theatre and concert tickets at the agencies; or simply sipping small beer by the roadside, beneath the trees, people-watching. There was one show in happy-go-lucky Belgrade that was completely free: the performance of the constable on point duty at one of the main intersections. He attracted a large, enthusiastic following by his elaborate repertory of ballet skills, with the kind of spontaneous exhibitionism one would never encounter in colder climes. Mason would gladly have lingered but for the urgency of his mission, and left the scene reflecting on the unexpected qualities of life under Communism.

He located the Embassy after a search among the official-looking buildings just off the main shopping centre, which was also, so he judged, the centre of restaurant and night life. He found a large, distinguished-looking building, set back a little from the street, with the Union Jack flying full mast from the roof. The Queen's birthday, he wondered? Or was it always there, proclaiming this bit of downtown Belgrade as genuine English territory? There was no mistaking the atmosphere of home as soon as he passed through the front door. A doorman in braided uniform greeted his arrival. There was a portrait of Her Majesty the Queen on the far wall, between two flights of spiral steps; a desk with yesterday's copy of *The Times*, several back numbers of *The Economist*, an old court circular. Even the smell of the place was somehow distinctly British, as if they had been frying sausages for lunch.

"Lost your passport, sir?" enquired the doorman, using his stock greeting.

Mason shook his head. If only it were as simple as that, instead of chasing shadows again, some of them inside his own head—those vague theories and forebodings he had carried with him all the long walk from the *Orsova*, relieved only by the total unexpectedness and incongruity of a dancing traffic constable.

"I wish to speak to the ambassador," he began, unsure if that was the correct protocol, but determined to get action from the top.

"You'll be lucky mate," the doorman said. "The ambassador's gone home on leave until the middle of September. Now your best bet would be the First Secretary, who's in full charge in his absence, but unfortunately he is not available until tomorrow, if you can wait that long. He was called down to the coast to sort out some problem with a group of tourists. You wouldn't believe what difficulties some people get themselves into!"

"Then whom can I see?" he asked, growing anxious about the time. Magda's guided tour would be over in another hour.

"I shall inform the Second Secretary at once," the doorman said. "If you would care to take a seat?" He indicated a bench by the newspaper rack. Mason took down *The Times* and found the report on the Third Test. He became so engrossed in it that he did not at first notice the neat diplomatic figure, dressed in pin-stripes, towering over him and smiling beneficently. The detective felt at once reassured by his presence.

"In a spot of trouble?" asked Mr. Charles Grayling, Second Secretary of the Belgrade embassy, seeing in Mason a stranded tourist.

"Is there somewhere we can talk privately?"

"Follow me," said Grayling, already several large strides ahead of him on his way to a large musty office heavily shuttered against the strong afternoon sun, and with an electric cooling fan revolving noisily overhead. "Now you may tell me what is the matter."

"It concerns one of your own men, rather than me personally," Mason explained. "A junior employee of the Foreign Office in London. His name is Michael Woolcot, and he is a member of our tour party."

"I am afraid I do not follow," said the secretary. "Which tour are you referring to?"

"The Danube cruise, from Vienna to the Black Sea."

The official's eyes lit up unexpectedly, showing a distinct strain of humour. "And our man Woolcot has gone overboard, has he?" he asked, jokingly. "Have to fish him out, eh?"

Mason patiently explained the sequence of events which had led to his presence at the embassy. Charles Grayling, much absorbed by the crease in his pin-stripes, grew increasingly attentive and concerned. He thought in silence for a while after Mason had finished.

"But surely this would be a matter for the local police, Mr. Mason?"

"The ship's captain has already gone to report the matter in that quarter," Mason explained. "I was simply acting on the assumption that Mr. Woolcot reported to the Budapest embassy, after he had been left behind at Castle Hill."

"That can quickly be ascertained, Mr. Mason," Grayling explained. "I'll put a call through right now." He picked up the telephone on his desk, spoke something in Serbo-Croat which Mason did not understand, then replaced the receiver to await the return call. He folded his arms and looked thoughtfully at Mason, as if phrasing to himself a rather delicate question.

"Do you think, Mr. Mason," he asked, eventually. "I mean, have you any grounds for believing that Mr. Woolcot may have been mixed up in anything illegal? It would be surprising in a member of the diplomatic corps, and exceedingly foolish, but there have unfortunately been precedents. Only last year, for example . . ."

"You mean profiteering, black-marketing or something like that?" Mason replied, dubiously. "I should consider that entirely out of the question. Mr. Woolcot struck me as being a particularly honest and serious young man."

"Appearances can be deceptive," Grayling said, without conviction.

The telephone gave a sharp ring, much accentuated by the limp humidity of the room; as if it alone had life. Grayling picked up the receiver and spoke into it.

"Trying to trace somebody by the name of Woolcot," he said. "He might have reported to your office." His expression told Mason the opposite. "Then listen," Grayling continued. "There's a party by the name of Woolcot who went missing in Budapest yesterday. "He's a passenger on board the *Orsova*, but he failed to report back to the ship. He was expected here in Belgrade, but he did not show up. Get on to the state police for us, will you? He can't simply have vanished into thin air. You'll call back in an hour? Very well. Will await your reply."

Grayling turned to Mason with a shrug. "What time does the boat sail?" he asked.

"Ten p.m., Central European time."

The official studied his watch. "That gives us about five hours," he said, "to have him back on board."

"I wish you luck," Mason said.

"I shouldn't worry too much about this if I were you," he went on, noting Mason's concern. "Enjoy your holiday and leave this to us; it's our line of business. Tourists often get into funny scrapes.

Only last month we had a case of mistaken identity. A perfectly ordinary English housewife from Chelmsford was arrested on suspicion of being a foreign agent. Took us weeks to sort that one out."

"Then we'll be lucky if we see Mr. Woolcot at all, this side of Vienna," Mason said, thinking out the full implications of that.

"Frankly, one can never tell," the Secretary said. "Good luck with your sightseeing. Belgrade is really a most fascinating city, if you don't mind a lot of modern architecture. Literally thrown up it was, in a couple of decades."

"Hadn't noticed," Mason confessed, without much of an eye for architectural detail. "You might direct me to the Ethnographical Museum. I understand it is well worth a visit."

The Second Secretary accompanied Mason as far as the outside door. "Turn left by the church of St. Alexandr Nevski," he instructed. "Walk along Franzuska Street as far as July 7th Street. You'll see it facing you. Good luck, and bon voyage."

"Cheers," Mason said, parting as ever with high impressions of the diplomatic corps. He wondered afterwards if he shouldn't have had Grayling contact Harrington; but surely that was premature. With a bit of luck Mike Woolcot might even now be back on board the *Orsova*, kicking his heels while the others returned. He was both amused and intrigued at Grayling's reference to a woman, feeling little doubt that it wasn't the same one as his unconventional table companion at the Hotel Vlad. What was *her* interest in his paperback guide? What was Ziegler's interest, other than an antiquarian one, in Woolcot's first edition, the one with the expensive plates? He continued along Franzuska Street, found the heat oppressive and paused thirstily at the pavement tables of the Café Kranj.

He sat down, ordered chilled beer and took out Woolcot's copy of *Bannerman's Guide*, examining it now, not for the tourist information for which it was so famous, but for some clue to its obvious importance for two rather strange, if not actually suspicious, characters whom he had encountered in the course of the last two days. He pushed his slim ball-point pen firmly into the spine, half-expecting some compromising material, special film or coded message for example, to nose its guilty way out of the opposite end. Nothing came, nor was there any indication either in the binding or in the text to suggest that this particular copy of the guide was anything more than it was supposed to be. No secret panels, no false back, no micro dots. With a rueful smile he placed the book on the table, sipped his beer and watched the relaxed and friendly natives stroll up and down July 7th Street, one of the main thoroughfares of central Belgrade. Poor Mike Woolcot was missing out on all this, on account of his over-enthusiasm for military architecture. And if he half expected a certain bespectacled American to cross from a nearby table and express keen interest in his first edition, he was disappointed. Or rather, he was relieved. There was nobody remotely fitting her description in the vicinity of the Café Kranj.

There would be time, he decided, for only a brief visit to the Ethnographical Museum, since he was to meet Clare Dyment within the hour and take her to dinner. He rose slowly, in the heat all movements were slow, carefully crossed the street and entered the sepulchral cool of the Museum interior, heading first for the collection on Serbian costume, customs and domestic architecture, if for no other reason than its location in the main hall to the right. He began at the Middle Ages, went through the Renaissance into modern times, and was in the act of contemplating a particularly fine example of nineteenth-century porcelain before becoming aware that Mrs. Walter B. Aveling was watching it, two steps behind him.

"Perfectly charming, isn't it, Mr. Mason?" she said, engagingly, discounting the look of astonishment on the detective's face. "There is an exact replica of it, as a matter of fact, in the Science Museum of Man. Except that the colouring does not seem half so authentic. Don't you think the glazing, especially on the floral motifs, is utterly breathtaking, Mr. Mason?"

"You followed me in here," he said, petulantly, recovering from his initial shock. "In fact, you have been following me all the way down the Danube River since I left Vienna. Now perhaps you will tell me why?"

"That is unfair, Mr. Mason," the American said, "and it is not true. I followed you in from Franzuska Street, because it is less conspicuous than on the sidewalk."

"You didn't follow me from Budapest?"

"I have a roving commission throughout the Eastern bloc. I am here on business, and when I saw you at the Kranj—I was on the inside, recording folk-music—I naturally wished to return your book. The one I borrowed rather naughtily from you in Budapest."

"You *borrowed* the book?" he asked, incredulously.

Mrs. Aveling nodded, fixing him with a rather disconcerting, roguishly disarming smile. At the same time she produced what he immediately recognised as his own purloined paperback guide from the depths of a large shoulder bag which also carried her cassette recorder.

"I was rather hoping that you would agree to exchange it for the book you are now carrying in your jacket pocket." And seeing the look of bewilderment on Mason's face, she continued: "I agree it is a far more valuable edition, Mr. Mason, and I am not proposing anything so crude as a straightforward swop. I will pay you well for it, much more than its actual worth, in sterling, dollars, roubles or forints. Whatever you please." She was already delving inside her shoulder bag, when Mason protested.

"My dear Mrs. Aveling," he began, as gallantly as he could, without failing to see the humorous side of things. "How could I possibly exchange my book for my book? In any case, the first edition is not mine to sell. It belongs to a Mr. Michael Woolcot." He did not say what had become of Woolcot, for he did not really know; nor did he think it was any business of the ubiquitous Mrs. Walter B. Aveling, of Minneapolis, Budapest and Belgrade.

The woman faltered, stunned by the unexpected setback. All the warmth and geniality drained from her face, her lips curled in a look of mortified defeat. Recovering her poise quickly, however, she said: "In that case I shall have to conduct negotiations with Mr. Woolcot personally. Is he now on board the *Orsova?*"

Mason shrugged helplessly. What could he say? This woman, for urgent reasons of her own, was determined to get her hands on Woolcot's book. Since she was American, he felt in some mysterious way that he should help her as much as possible.

"You could try the British Embassy in Budapest," he suggested, with the odd feeling he would meet Mrs. Aveling again in Bucharest, without really knowing why.

"Budapest!" she exclaimed. "What on earth is he doing there?"

CHAPTER FIVE

B y the time George Mason met up with Clare Dyment on the corner of Dunavska Street it was turned seven o'clock and the sun was already setting somewhere over the Adriatic. They strolled along the river embankment past the *Orsova* and round the broad sweep of the Zoological Gardens, stopping only to ascertain what they both instinctively felt, that Mike Woolcot had not so far returned from Budapest to resume his cruise. The Intourist guide shook her head negatively, from her station on the foredeck, so that the couple did not even stop to board the ship. Magda indicated her watch, as if there was still time. There remained in fact three hours before their departure from Belgrade.

Clare had a wild, disconcerted look in her eyes, which the detective at first attributed to her concern and anxiety over Woolcot. It was not until they were well on their way to dinner at the Zagreb Restaurant, housed on a converted paddle steamer in the Sava River, that she explained to him the circumstances in which her copy of *Bannerman's Guide* had been stolen from her; snatched from her grasp in the crowded porch of the Church of St. Alexandr Nevski, their first stopping point on the guided tour. In the dim light she had caught only the vaguest glimpse of the thief, as he disappeared quickly down the church steps and merged with the pavement crowd. Her impression was that he was a Yugoslav rather than a West European, a detail which the detective found highly significant.

"There seems to be an incredible amount of interest in the works of Auguste Bannerman," he remarked, "throughout the entire Eastern bloc." Feeling suddenly protective he slipped his arm about her waist, a gesture which she did not repel.

"It's not the value of the book," she explained, "but the nastiness of the act. It cost me all of sixty-five pence in the basement of Foyle's bookshop. It almost ruined my afternoon."

"Curious how there came to be three copies of the same book on board the same boat," Mason said, thinking aloud. "It's not as if there aren't other guides, Nagel's or Fodor's, for example. Hope it didn't spoil things too much for you."

"The conducted tour was excellent," Clare said, perking up at the memory. "We took in the Cathedral, two baroque churches, the University, the National Museum and the Fresco Gallery."

"Quite an itinerary in two hours," Mason observed, feeling envious. "But you did not call at the Ethnographical Museum, on July 7th Street."

"How do you know that?"

"I was there myself, and I was hoping you would arrive."

The girl flushed perceptibly, in the red-orange glow of the setting sun reflected in the turgid pool of the Danube, lined on one bank with official buildings, on the other by the trees and shrubs of the Zoological Gardens. It was the first time Mason had said anything personal like that, although she must have guessed the direction of his feelings from the diplomatic silence he maintained in respect of her civil service colleague. She gently detached herself from his protecting arm and said, almost as a challenge:

"You did not tell me how you fared at the Embassy. Was there any news of Mike?"

"I was going to wait until we had eaten dinner before telling you," he replied. "But since you ask, Budapest have no knowledge of Michael Woolcot. I was in touch with them by phone again just before we met, but there was still no news."

"You know, George," she said, pressing closer to him again. "I have a feeling that this is not an ordinary cruise at all. I have a creeping suspicion that something nasty is going to happen before very long. Perhaps it has already happened."

"Shall we eat dinner first, and then discuss it? Something else very interesting happened this afternoon, which I have not told you about."

The Zagreb restaurant loomed up suddenly round a bend in the path, a romantic-looking paddle steamer, festooned with fairy lights and with a small orchestra playing on the foredeck. In the balm of the subtropical evening, the sound first competed then merged with the noise of the crickets in the overhanging trees. Casually-dressed tourists strolled on and off, mingling with the native Serbs on the dancing square lit up beneath the trees. The air was heavy with scents, of the flowers, of the trees, of the wine and the exotic cuisine. The sort of ambiance he imagined would appeal to Mrs. Walter B. Aveling.

"Coming aboard?" he said, feeling suddenly like a tourist again, letting Mike Woolcot slip from his mind.

"Do you think I dare, George?" she enquired, with an oddly provocative glance at the bemused Mason.

"My treat, remember," he said, leading the way in an eager bound up the gangplank and into the cramped, archaic and rather musty interior of the ship's galley, which had been converted into a tastefully appointed restaurant. They found a table for two by one of the starboard portholes, ordered Chicken à la Kiev and a bottle of Riesling from the waitress in national dress, glanced enraptured at the water beneath them, with the dark shadows of ships plying by, from Budapest to the Black Sea.

"Isn't it romantic, George?" Clare whispered. "Just what I imagined a Danube cruise to be."

"The way the brochure describes it," Mason said, quoting from memory. *"Languid summer evenings by the river; exotic cuisine; local colour."*

Clare laughed. At that moment he could tell she was supremely happy; a young girl enraptured by her first trip abroad. On the Danube, too; the most majestic of all rivers.

"I expect you've travelled a lot, George," she said, after a quiet moment in which they absorbed the atmosphere of the Zagreb. "I have that impression about you, although I know you so little."

Mason was diffident. "My work occasionally takes me abroad," he replied. "But not very often. That was why I came down here. To see something really different."

"And you like what you see?"

"If it wasn't for all the mystery going on. This thing about Mike. It makes me feel uneasy. And again, this afternoon . . ."

"You were going to tell me what happened."

They were interrupted by the serving of the meal, an exotically dressed fowl presented by an equally eye-catching waitress, in a costume that reminded Mason of something in the Ethnographical Museum. The wine waiter arrived simultaneously, and as Mason raised the sampler to his lips and glanced about the room, he half expected his eyes to be met in the dim candle-lit depths by those of Mrs. Aveling. But he discerned no recognisable face.

"I met Mrs. Aveling again," he said.

Clare merely looked puzzled. Her attention was more than half absorbed by the meal.

"Mrs. Who?" she asked.

"Mrs. Aveling," Mason repeated. "The woman who took my paperback from the Hotel Vlad."

"You didn't tell me her name," Clare said. "But whatever excuse did she give for her odd behaviour?"

"None. She wanted to exchange it for the copy I was carrying. It was Mike's copy."

The girl's eyes opened wide in disbelief. "You're kidding, George," she decided. "Having me on."

"The honest truth," Mason protested. "She followed me into the Museum and proposed the deal. I have the feeling she follows me everywhere. She certainly turns up wherever the *Orsova* docks. She's almost bound to be in Bucharest."

The girl appeared to concentrate on eating her chicken. After a while she said, simply: "What Herr Ziegler said must be correct. Mike's is a rare first edition, a collector's item. That explains the sudden interest in it. We ought to hold out for the highest bidder."

Mason glanced sternly at her, like a schoolmaster at a wayward pupil.

"Does that explain to you why an unknown Serb should suddenly snatch your copy in broad daylight and make off with it down Franzuska Street?"

"I suppose it doesn't," Clare said, more soberly.

"It doesn't explain to me either why an obviously wealthy American woman should offer so much money for mine, or rather for Mike's."

He savoured the wine, waiting for a more intelligent response.

"At a guess," Clare said, eventually, "one of the books has a more than antiquarian value."

"Exactly," he said. "The question is which one? Certainly not mine. Must be yours or Mike's."

The girl experienced a sudden feeling of unease. She lowered her eyes without answering. The gay, holiday atmosphere of the Zagreb, the romantic associations of the river at night, the blurred outlines of boats passing to and fro, the wail of sirens, the dimly perceived human shapes on their decks, took on a more sinister pall. Perhaps for the first time she truly feared that something bad had happened to Mike Woolcot in the Kossuth Tower, all those miles back along the river, as if she had known him in a previous life. Budapest was now overlaid with later, more vivid images. Her present was Belgrade, the Zagreb restaurant, the mature and dependable George Mason.

"Who was with you when the book was stolen?" he suddenly asked.

"Why, Anton Ziegler of course. He was there from the moment we left the boat until I met you."

Mason's brows knit in concentration. "That could be significant in itself," he said.

"How do you mean?" Clare said, looking alarmed.

"I mean that he was also with Mike Woolcot just before he disappeared in Budapest."

"Now you have lost me," Clare said, with an air of impatience at his opaque line of reasoning. "I got the impression that he was interested in practising his English. The Swiss are like that. Very practical in their approach to life."

"He could have been used as a marker," Mason suggested. "To indicate to some third party precisely who, among the members of the *Orsova* tour, was carrying *Bannerman's Guide*."

Clare poised a forkful of succulent chicken before pink parted lips, then let it down carefully onto the plate, into the deep, rich butter sauce.

"Do you really expect me to believe that, Mr. Mason?" she asked, suddenly reverting to his surname. "That someone as kind and attentive and courteous as Herr Ziegler, who took immense pains to explain all sorts of things on the guided tour, was really only lining me up to be robbed?"

"I was going to order the cherry strudel for dessert," he said, abruptly changing the subject. "Will you join me?"

"If you will also order me a strong Turkish coffee!"

Mason smiled to himself. He had made a faux pas, but there was still time to recover from it. He ordered strudels for two and gazed out of the porthole at the swell of the waves caused by a passing ship. The Danube was not blue, he decided, but black. Then he remembered to phone Grayling again. He excused himself, rose from the table and crossed the floor rather uncertainly, on account of the wine and the slight tilt at which the Zagreb was anchored. On shore was a public call box, and the Second Secretary had told him he would be working late. But there was still no news of Woolcot from the Budapest embassy. The Hungarian State Police, for their part, were either unable or unwilling to give information. The official line was that Woolcot was lost, and a search had been mounted in the district of Castle Hill and the winding streets of old Buda. Grayling appeared to hint that he might have defected, gone over to the other side with secret information. Such cases, usually premeditated, always took one by surprise. Mason did not quite know what to make of that, and he resolved not to mention it to Clare.

When he returned to the table, the girl had already forgotten her indignation over Ziegler and recovered her good humour. He shook his head when she enquired about Mike, noted the frown which puckered her brow and resolved to help her enjoy their evening together as much as possible. They joined the tight knot of dancers in the space between the tables and the orchestra. Clare yielded her slender form to his embrace. He felt the soft firm pressure of her body, the dampness of her skin beneath the thin cotton blouse. The river enveloped them, with its darkness, its silence, its mystery, its romance.

In a different part of the city, not far from where George Mason had spent part of his afternoon, a shadowy figure slipped unobtrusively along the south side of Franzuska Street. Keeping close to the perimeter of the Ethnographical Museum, he quickly reached the Café Kranj, arrested for a mere moment by the sharp sound of a ship's siren some distance behind him in the Danube River. His name was Janos, and he was a student in the Economics Faculty of the University. To supplement his student stipend, he had a profitable sideline making shady deals with tourists, trading in anything from shirts to wrist watches, buying foreign currency on the black market, and generally keeping on the wrong side of the law.

Mrs. Aveling had chosen a table well out of sight of the restaurant entrance, in a corner obscured by the small stage. For the Kranj was a well-known folklorist venue, and Mrs. Walter B. Aveling, in addition to her commercial and political interests, was an avid collector of anything from negro spirituals to Danube boat songs. Even as she sat waiting for the intrepid Janos to show up, she was sipping slivovitz and recording on her portable cassette player the relentless rhythms of a Macedonian dance. It compensated her to some extent for her feelings of disappointment and frustration at her encounters with the English tourist, Mason, whom she had carefully cultivated since he had left Vienna; and for her fruitless visit to the *Orsova* an hour ago in search of Mr. Woolcot.

Janos entered warily, keeping close to the wall and well outside the perimeter of light that illuminated the stage and the surrounding tables, comforted by the knowledge that at this time of year the restaurant was mainly visited by foreign tourists, who relegated the regular Bohemian element in Belgrade life to the more secluded cafés on the side streets. One could run into an informer anywhere, someone who might recognise him from the University, someone who would give his name to the police.

Mrs. Aveling—call me Betsy—placed a manicured finger to her lips to indicate silence, as he slid quietly into the seat beside her, towards the end of the Macedonian dance. When the music ceased and the dancers had left the floor to a resounding applause, she replaced her recorder in her shoulder bag with a gesture of satisfaction and smiled generously towards the student.

"Such lovely music," she said, with feeling. "The preservation of national culture is something of which your government must feel justly proud. Only this afternoon, at the Ethnographical Museum . . ."

"I brought the book," Janos said, impatiently sliding it from his pocket and placing it on the table. He was anxious to receive in exchange the coveted dollar bills which she had promised him, and which he could exchange very favourably against local currency.

The American removed her tinted spectacles and fixed him with a look almost of reproach, albeit of mild reproach, at his mercenariness. She then replaced them to examine the musty brown copy of *Bannerman's Guide* which Clare Dyment had purchased ten days ago at Foyle's Bookshop on Charing Cross Road. The carefully-bound, beautifully illustrated volume appeared to satisfy her brief inspection. She placed it securely alongside her cassette-recorder, in the depths of her shoulder bag.

"Of course, this is not worth very much by itself. You do understand that, don't you, my dear Janos?" She sat back to judge the effect of her words, hoping to acquire the article as cheaply as possible.

The young student appeared non-plussed, lowered his shaggy head, scratched and alternately smoothed his curls. It was difficult to tell whether he was offended, angry, or merely embarrassed.

"You told me ..." he began, impatiently.

"There are in fact two, almost identical, copies of this book," she explained. "But there are some differences. There is this one, which you enterprisingly, if rather brusquely, obtained from the English girl. You haven't told me where."

"The Church of St. Alexandr Nevski," he replied, puzzled by her ambivalence.

"Full credit to you, none the less, since you have evidently had more success than I." She paused and removed her spectacles again, so that her eyes appeared older, more tired. "And there is a second copy, which I myself have had the opportunity to observe in the hands of Mr. George Mason, also a passenger on the *Orsova* cruise."

"Which you were unable to persuade him to part with?" Janos asked in amused surprise.

The American emitted a sigh of exasperation.

"Unfortunately," she said, I do not possess your strong pair of heels. I could not effect what the British are apt to call a smash and grab."

"Persuasion didn't help?" he asked, twitching his fingers to suggest banknotes.

"The book was not his property to sell," she replied, sharply. "It is apparently the property of a Mr. Michael Woolcot, whom I found it impossible to trace earlier when I visited the ship. The

Intourist guide explained that he had been delayed in Budapest, but heaven knows how or why."

"Where does that place me?" Janos asked.

Mrs. Aveling reached nimbly into her shoulder bag, withdrew from it an alligator-skin purse, opened it and took out two bills of medium denomination. Pressing them into the student's hand, she said:

"Of course, this copy may well turn out to be the one we want. I shall examine it more closely later, away from prying eyes. If you are in luck, it will be worth considerably more than I am paying you this evening. Regard this, optimistically, as a payment on account. If, on the other hand, it turns out not to be the right one, then I am afraid, my dear Janos, that you will already have been very handsomely compensated for a secondhand guidebook, which I can see from the Foyle's marking cost only a few English pence."

Janos smiled ironically. He was not devoid of a certain sense of humour, and if in his impetuosity and desire for financial gain he had rated his achievement considerably higher than fifty U.S. dollars, he was not about to bite the hand that fed him. He agreed to the deal and arranged for a second encounter for tomorrow evening at the Zagreb. As he left, Mrs. Walter B. Aveling once more resumed her interest in the Macedonian dance.

CHAPTER SIX

G eorge Mason arrived late on deck the following morning, following his visit to the Zagreb Restaurant with Clare Dyment; so late, in fact, that he had to skip breakfast. He still expected to be ahead of the girl, whom he visualised as heavy-eyed and languid after their protracted encounter afterwards in her cabin on B-deck. He was doubly surprised to find her fresh as the morning and sitting in a deckchair alongside Mike Woolcot, enjoying iced drinks and earnest conversation, in company with Oliver Markham and Gayle Sumner. Clare flushed slightly at his appearance, as if remembering her indiscretions of the previous evening, and invited him to take his seat in the chair she had reserved for him on the opposite side to the resurrected civil servant.

"Surprise, surprise," Mason said coolly, wondering how on earth he had managed to materialise.

"Missed you at breakfast, George, old chap," Woolcot said, provocatively. "Making heavy water?"

Mason grinned, or rather grimaced, not at all in the mood for the other's peculiarly incisive sense of humour, but still with a certain qualified relief that he had showed up. It restored his sense of vacation.

"Welcome aboard," he said, as convincingly as he could. "We had almost given you up for lost. A recruit to the five-year plan."

"I told him," Clare said, "of all the trouble you have taken trying to find him. How you gave up your free time ashore to check with the Embassy. How the captain went to the police."

"You must at least let me buy you a drink," Mike offered, springing to his feet. To Mason he seemed remarkably cool and collected for a person who had been missing for two days in a police state.

"No need to rush off," Mason said, not relishing the thought of cold beer on an empty stomach. "I'll order a bite to eat when the waiter comes by."

"If you look this way now, high up there on the right," Oliver Markham was saying, "you will see the Tablet of Trajan."

"The what . . . ?" asked the trio in unison.

"It's a famous landmark," the teacher exclaimed excitedly, bringing his field glasses to bear on a particularly smooth piece of masonry set high in the face of the sheer rock. "You can almost make out the inscription."

"You read it for us," Clare said, weary as Mason was of the touristics.

Woolcot smiled. He could sense Mason's eagerness to hear his story; but it would wait until the schoolmaster was through.

"It states," declared Markham, pedantically: *Trajan Augustus, Tribune and Father of His Country, has Conquered the Mountain and the River.* "That would be an approximate translation."

His efforts received a polite handclap from the English party, which was sufficient to raise the eyes of Herr Anton Ziegler, who was playing deck chess with a compatriot.

"That's what it says," Mason remarked, impatiently. "But why is it there? That's what I should like to know."

"To mark a famous Roman victory, I should think," Gayle Sumner said, giving Oliver moral support.

"The Romans were all over here," Woolcot said. "The Province of Transdanubia."

During the night the Danube had flowed beyond the fertile plains east of Belgrade into spectacularly barren mountain scenery rising sheer from the banks of the river, so that the *Orsova* seemed hemmed in amidst rapid, swirling currents. Ahead was the famous Iron Gate, the gorge which opened the passage through the Transylvanian Alps onto the lowlands of Rumania; a passage the *Orsova* would navigate, Markham informed them, by means of a specially cut canal. The Tablet of Trajan was set high up in the rock-face of the Defile of Kazan, a stretch of the Danube noted for swirling waters over still pools which bred sturgeon. The Germans were up front with their Ziesses flashing; and that was certainly where the English party would have been were it not for the surprise re-appearance of their compatriot at the breakfast table.

"You were going to say . . ." Mason prompted.

"To cut a long story short," Woolcot began, loathe to cover the same ground again, but feeling that he owed something to Mason for his trouble. "I travelled down to Belgrade by train from Budapest—you know, the famous Orient Express that was. I just managed to scramble aboard this tub before it set sail. It was late and I assumed you had all turned in."

Mason exchanged glances with Clare, but she quickly averted her eyes.

"Tell him what happened in the Kossuth Tower," Gayle prompted, with girlish excitement.

"You won't believe this, George, old chap," said the civil servant. "The Kossuth Tower must be some kind of classified monument. Apparently there was a notice on the wall, in Hungarian only, absolutely forbidding entry to tourists. It was probably an oversight that the portcullis was left open. I strayed inside and . . . Bob's your uncle!"

"You mean you trespassed on restricted ground and got yourself arrested?"

"Right first time, George," Woolcot said, with heavy irony. "Absolutely correct."

"And you were formally charged?"

"The Kossuth Tower," Woolcot went on to explain, apparently houses a permanent exhibition of some highly sensitive military electronics. Just imagine it! They assumed, since I had my camera with me, that I wished to take photographs. I was promptly hauled off to the police station and charged with espionage."

"There was a similar case in Greece," Gayle recalled, "some years ago. They arrested plane spotters, a couple of young boys."

"I remember that," Oliver said.

To Mason it sounded incredible, until he reflected on the way the official mind worked behind the Iron Curtain: tourist, camera, sensitive material, prison. It was an all-too-logical progression.

Woolcot did not seem in the least ruffled by his adventure. In Mason's experience, that might indicate an unusual degree of sangfroid, or complete fabrication. On balance, he decided temporarily in favour of the young man, now basking in the admiration and anxious concern of the entire English party, and particularly of Clare Dyment.

"Weren't you able to apply for representation by the British Embassy?" he asked in some surprise, thinking it odd there had been no official knowledge of the matter, such as could have been relayed to the Belgrade Embassy.

"The matter was never raised," Woolcot said. "By the time they had developed the film in my camera and interrogated me through a police interpreter, I'd already been in prison—just a locked room with a bed, really—for a day and a half. Suddenly they let me go. Just like that."

"They must have believed your story," Clare said, with relief. "And decided not to press charges."

"I did tell them I was a member of the Diplomatic Service," Woolcot explained. "That might have made them nervous of official complications and wary of jeopardising good relations. I don't know. Quite out of the blue they said I was free to go. They gave me a train ticket to Belgrade, drove me to the railway station and made sure I got aboard. So here I am."

"You've had a remarkable escape," Gayle Sumner said, with feeling.

"I think I'll have that drink you promised me," Mason said. "Or perhaps I should really buy you one!"

"Forget it," Woolcot said, genially. "I have to thank you for trailing all over Belgrade on my behalf. That was very decent of you, George."

Mason made a dismissive gesture. He would have done the same for any one of them.

"What will it be?" Woolcot asked.

"Lager," the detective said. "Danish"

"That must be Trajan's bridge, or what is left of it," Oliver Markham remarked from the ship's rail. "You can see the remains of the piles. He must have built a road out here, to carry out his campaign."

The English party smiled to each other. They had returned in spirit from the sinister associations of the Kossuth Tower to the Danube Cruise. They raised and touched glasses, toasted the Emperor Trajan in rather facetious fashion, mainly for Oliver's benefit; while Mason relaxed into the depths of his canvas chair, sipped his beer slowly and thought his own thoughts, while the grandiose scenery of the Iron Gate loomed up on either hand.

Over lunch talk turned on Clare Dyment's misadventure at the Church of St. Alexandr Nevski, something which had been let slip in the general concern over Mike Woolcot. The theft of her book, the civil servant declared, should have been reported at once to the police, despite its low value. And Gayle Sumner wondered if there were not some kind of jinx on the English party.

"Merely a strange series of coincidences," George Mason remarked in reassurance, while sinking his fork into the soft flesh of a sturgeon cutlet.

"You forgot to mention," Clare remarked, "that your paperback was taken also, from the Hotel Vlad."

"What on earth is all this?" remarked Oliver Markham. "Soon no one will dare go ashore carrying anything! Are the natives so deprived of literature?"

His rhetorical question went unanswered, except for a smile from George Mason.

"It doesn't sound like coincidence, George," Gayle said, mysteriously.

"It's as if one of the books contains secret information. The interested party, whoever he or she may be, does not yet know which of the three copies in our possession is the right one."

"*Two* copies," Clare emphasised. "Don't forget that mine has not yet been returned.

"If Mike's adventure could be interpreted in the same light," Gayle suggested, "it might explain a lot."

The civil servant moved his napkin to his lips to suppress a slight yawn.

"There I am afraid I must disappoint you," he said, rather pompously. "I was not even carrying my guidebook when I went ashore in Budapest. Remember, Oliver, I left it with you?"

"That is correct," the geography master agreed. "And I locked it in my cabin."

Gayle Sumner's line of reasoning much intrigued the detective, for it had the same conclusion he had reached himself. Mike Woolcot, however, was sceptical and threw cold water on it.

"A thief will snatch anything he considers of the least value," he said. "Especially in a crowded place. You are lucky he did not snatch your purse. And as for George's book, that was simply a mistake, rectified later by the American woman."

"I don't think the matter can be dismissed so lightly as that," Gayle insisted. "You might all of you think this is ridiculous, but I have my own interpretation of what has happened."

"Oh?" said all three at once. "An original theory?"

The girl flushed slightly at the teasing.

"I was thinking, Michael, that there might be some connection between your work at the Foreign Office and the disappearance of the books," she explained. "Unknown to yourself, you might be acting as courier, for something concealed inside the book."

Woolcot exploded into laughter so loud that it attracted momentary attention from other parts of the deck.

"Do you find that so preposterous?" Gayle asked, tersely.

"I told you I was not even carrying my Bannerman when I was arrested," Woolcot insisted. "What possible connection could there be between the two?"

Mason smiled, intrigued at the difference in opinion. He almost inclined towards Gayle's view. But there were no hard facts to support it; and he had examined Woolcot's copy himself thoroughly for any tell-tale signs.

"Might I put one question, Mr. Woolcot?" he asked, "before we forget about mysteries and concentrate on enjoying our cruise."

"Be my guest," Mike said, equably.

"How did you acquire your Bannerman? I bought mine at Smith's and Clare obtained hers at Foyle's. Merely as a matter of interest."

Woolcot seemed not to have expected the question and fidgeted a little with his fork before answering.

"It was loaned to me, as a personal favour," he said, carefully, "by a fellow diplomat in London. He used it himself for this same cruise two years ago. Do you see anything sinister in that?" The last remark was thrown out almost as a challenge.

"A British diplomat, Mr. Woolcot?" Mason persisted.

"An American, as a matter of fact, Mr. Mason," the other replied coolly. "If that makes any difference. We are on the same side, technically at least."

Mason found his last remark significant. Woolcot had unconsciously gone on the defensive. What had he to be defensive about? His association with American diplomats? One American might well be involved with another. He thought of Mrs. Walter B. Aveling and it seemed at least a possibility that she and Woolcot's London friend could be in some way connected; that the book Woolcot was carrying could, unknown to Woolcot himself, contain some information of value to the Americans. That posed the interesting question of whether Mrs. Aveling had some connection with intelligence work; whether, in fact, her roving commission throughout the Eastern bloc was not sponsored by the CIA.

"I was merely indulging myself, Mike old man," he said, sensing that he had gone too far, but pleased to turn the tables for once on Woolcot.

Clare Dyment smiled uneasily, sensing that the rivalry between them was on her account. She distracted their attention to the strong sunshine through the portholes of the dining-room. After their excellent meal of river fish they anticipated no further excitement until the *Orsova* docked at Giurgiu the following day; it was the nearest port of call for Bucharest.

"While we're on the subject," Woolcot asked. "Which of you has *my* book?"

"I do," Mason replied. "I'll get it for you when we go on deck."

"I shall have to wear it chained to my wrist," the other remarked, "whenever we go ashore. Either that, or leave it in my cabin, where it will be of no use."

"That might not be a bad idea," Mason quipped.

CHAPTER SEVEN

In a rear room of the American Embassy in Dionisei Lupu Street, whose tall windows overlooked the courtyard of the Museum of the History of Bucharest, Mrs. Walter B. Aveling sat in a straight-backed leather armchair, waiting for the Legal Attaché, Mr. Everett Hodge, to conclude his conversation with Belgrade. At arm's length in well-manicured fingers, she held a Filter Long in a black-and-gold cigarette holder. She drew it languidly to her lips, on account of the heat, while her eyes took in, in turn, the bald pate of Mr. Everett Hodge, creased with deep furrows, the mesmerising revolutions of the overhead electric fan and the sallow, careworn features of a Rumanian woman looking down from a Museum window balcony onto the courtyard beneath. She rose from the chair, still carrying the cigarette, smoothed the wrinkles from the skirt of her white two-piece and replenished her glass from a decanter of local wine not dissimilar to sherry, which the official kept on his desk.

There was a sudden silence in the room, punctuated by the low hum and occasional tick of the revolving fan. Hodge had concluded his business on the phone and was glancing towards her expectantly, but she said nothing until she had regained her seat, with her drink and her cigarette.

"Well, Betsy?" he enquired, his face lighting into an ironic smile. "How was it in Belgrade?"

"Interesting," replied the woman, for whom any kind of vocal exertion in the heat seemed an effort. "But inconclusive."

"You failed to find the book?"

Mrs. Aveling reached down into her shoulder bag, which she had placed on the polished parquet floor beside her, and drew out

Clare Dyment's copy of the guide-book. "It's the wrong one," she explained, showing it to him. "But it was worth fifty dollars and a couple of drinks to find that out."

Hodge pursed his lips, frowning slightly. "Charge it to expenses," he said. He read the message behind those tired eyes, which told him she had had enough, that leave was overdue, and she was ready to return home. The knowledge that he recognised that fact, even if he could do nothing about it, seemed to spur her to renewed enthusiasm.

"This afternoon, when the party arrives in Bucharest, we shall make no mistakes," she said.

"Supposing the Bannerman is not brought ashore?" Hodge asked, nervously.

Mrs. Aveling sighed. "In that case I shall have no choice but to go down to Mammaia. The book cannot possibly go farther than that, and Bucharest may well be its last port of call. A pity about Belgrade; it would have saved me a deal of trouble."

"You are quite sure that is the wrong copy you have there?"

"You can see for yourself, Everett," she explained, holding it up again. "Empty."

"No trace of any photograph?"

"A photograph or negative, whichever it is, could only have been concealed carefully rolled up into the spine. If it was there originally, it has since been taken out."

"By Mr. Woolcot, do you think?"

Mrs. Aveling appeared uncertain. "He may be aware of its existence, I am not sure."

"You are certain this is not some kind of red herring? A false trail to waste our time and resources, while our enemies concentrate on something else?"

"Would I have come this far down if I thought that, Everett? I was doing very good business in Budapest, with synthetic lipsticks!"

"If you should need some assistance . . ."

Mrs. Aveling smiled and shook her head, as if to imply that there were things a woman could do more easily than a man. She had already recovered two of the books, and anticipated no undue difficulty about the third, provided that it resurfaced at the right moment.

"I merely wished to make arrangements for the transfer-on of the material once it comes into our possession. The State Department is most anxious for its retrieval."

"Did they tell you why?"

"Do they ever give reasons, Everett? You know them as well as I do. What I do know is that Woolcot was loaned the guidebook by someone at our London embassy, just before the start of the *Orsova* cruise. That someone, I understand, has also been under recent surveillance by MI5."

Hodge whistled. "Quite an interesting kettle of fish," he commented. "Whatever you do, Betsy, don't take unnecessary risks, keep in touch and inform us of your movements in advance. If you get in trouble, we'll know in which direction to look."

With that understanding, Mrs. Aveling left the embassy and walked along Dionisei Lupu Street, as far as the intersection with Rosetti Boulevard, crossed and entered through the front entrance of the Hotel Florescu. At the rear was a large garden-restaurant, with tables and chairs set out beneath the palms. She took a seat by the wall, ordered a glass of furmint, and withdrew her cassette recorder from the depths of her shoulder bag. On it she registered the performance of a singer from Oltenia, a valuable addition to the collection of folk music with which she would regale the members of the Midwest Musicological Society on the occasion of her annual Fall lecture. The background was filled out with the noise of bathers in the outdoor swimming pool, complete with simulated waves and a diving board. The amenities of the Florescu confirmed her already favourable view of life in the Rumanian capital. But who were these people so unabashedly enjoying themselves, while others bore the burden of the day and the heat? They were not all foreign tourists.

She had chosen the restaurant of the Florescu for another reason: it was the luncheon stop and starting point on the tour of Bucharest for the *Orsova* passengers, due to arrive any moment now by bus from Giurgiu, where the ship had berthed. She was half way through her *soupe paysanne* when her attention was arrested by the sudden fluster of the hotel waiters, as they shepherded the large tour party now seen to emerge through the French windows at the hotel rear. She recognised the curiously ambling figure of the stubborn Englishman she had met in Belgrade, the same personage whom she had also briefly encountered in Budapest. He was at the centre of a group of unmistakably English tourists, younger than himself, who now occupied the table by the fountain. Her eyes scanned them separately for sight of the guidebook, fixing at once on Mike Woolcot, who had quite innocently placed it on the table in front of him as if about to consult it for his visit to Bucharest.

It struck her as odd that the young man did not afterwards rejoin his companions outside the front entrance to the hotel, but proceeded instead along Rosetti Boulevard in the direction of Piata 1848, at an unhurried gait, as if merely intent on imbibing local atmosphere and observing the antics, unspectacular enough in the afternoon heat, of the local people. She was so concerned to keep him in view as he wove in and out of the pavement crowd that she failed to notice the other Englishman, George Mason, bringing up the rear. He had also forgone the opportunity of a guided tour of the city, and with it the pleasure of Clare's company, to keep close tabs on Woolcot. There had come a point mid-way through luncheon when Mason's curiosity had got the better of him, through an intriguing combination of circumstances: Woolcot's announcement of his intention to explore the city alone, and his sudden awareness of Mrs. Walter B. Aveling watching them all closely from the far side of the swimming pool.

Perhaps it was simply that he had not found the civil servant's story one hundred per cent credible, regarding his absence in Budapest. Perhaps it was simply that his determination to uncover a mystery was stronger than his interest, not very great at the best of times, in Museums of Ethnography, Socialist-Realist Art, Cathedrals, Libraries and sundry stock attractions, in all of which Bucharest would be as richly endowed as either of the Danube cities they had already visited. He willingly bore the heat of the city streets, the dust and the pervasiveness of traffic fumes, which in the broad sunlight caused an unpleasant smog. It crossed his mind that Mike Woolcot was on his way to meet someone; there was a certain purposefulness in his gait once he was clear of the hotel.

After continuing for some time along the main boulevard, the trail ended at the Church of St. Georghe, on the Piata 1848. The square formed the core of the well-preserved mediaeval centre of Bucharest, and from his point of entry Mason saw Woolcot mount the church steps and disappear through the darkness of the porch. Mrs. Aveling, at pains to keep up with his normal walking pace, had only narrowly closed the gap between them, when she too disappeared inside the church, clutching the broken strap of her shoulder bag. Mason broke into a sprint, perspiring freely in the heat until the welcome cool of the porch engulfed him. He saw Woolcot kneeling up front among other shadowy figures. The interior was dim, filled with incense and a monotonous chant from the faithful who queued to press pious lips against a golden reliquary. They were elderly people, Mason noted, as they had been in the churches of Budapest and Belgrade. He peered more closely at the reliquary: it contained a black and withered hand—the hand of St. Georghe? He shuddered, but what was Woolcot doing up there, on his knees and for all the world like some pious Orthodox? And where was Mrs. Aveling, the ubiquitous American? He had seen her enter, but she had now disappeared from sight.

Mason's eyes peeled the darkness. Woolcot remained motionless, head slightly bowed as if in prayer, while the chant droned on, with the peculiar ebb and flow of liturgical music. The black-shawled women filed past him reverently, returning from the reliquary. Mason instinctively knelt and crossed himself; it seemed the thing to do. And as his eyes raised again towards Woolcot, he was aware of someone kneeling next to him, their shoulders adjacent in the darkness. Some kind of contact, was his first reaction, as renewed suspicion arose in his mind regarding Woolcot's version of events in Budapest. A contact, met here by pre-arrangement, for handing on the material contained in the guidebook! The conclusion leapt at him, though he could see little, from the dark interior of the church.

But there was no sign of Mrs. Aveling and he began to grow anxious on her account. Several doors leading to confessionals opened off the side aisles. Had she entered one of them? Or was she observing Woolcot from some vantage point invisible to him? Mason flattened himself against a pillar as Woolcot rose from his pew and strode quickly down the nave. His companion stayed put. Without glancing to either side, Woolcot walked out of the church clutching his Bannerman in his hand. It seemed a safe guess that he would now complete his sight-seeing in Bucharest and return for tea to the garden restaurant of the Hotel Florescu, before catching the bus back with the rest to the waiting boat.

The contact waited for Woolcot to get clear, before rising to his feet, genuflecting and crossing himself in the manner of a pious Orthodox, and hurrying down the north aisle past the pillar against which George Mason had been standing. He caught a glimpse of the man's face, the swarthy complexion of a Rumanian, which would be difficult to distinguish in a crowd. Forgetting all about Mrs. Aveling, who had so strangely disappeared, he decided to follow Woolcot's contact on the assumption that he was carrying the secret contents of the book. At all costs he must see where the contact went next. But by the time he had regained the Church steps, the figure was already half way across the Piata, heading north towards the Calei Victoriei.

Mason broke into a laboured sprint, eventually closing the gap undetected amid the lively jostling crowd of the main boulevard. He then lost sight of him for a while in the vicinity of the Piata Republicii, only to see him double back on the other side of the street, as if unsure of his direction. He finally stopped outside a large stone building, and with a glance up at the tall, curtained windows hurried inside. Mason was deeply intrigued, but in no mind to follow him in. He would wait at the café opposite and see how long he remained inside. His watch told him there was less than an hour before tea in the garden of the Hotel Florescu, and the long trek back to the waiting boat It would arouse Woolcot's suspicions if he were late. He ordered strong coffee and sipped it slowly, his eyes scanning the stark, soulless structure opposite.

"That building," he enquired of the waiter in German, the lingua franca of all the countries through which they had travelled. "What is it?"

The waiter eyed him nervously, and had already moved on to the next table before turning to answer, under his breath: "Ministry of Information."

Mason smiled quietly to himself. The knowledge confirmed all his suspicions of Woolcot. There *was* something in the guidebook after all! Something he himself had been unable to detect, unless Woolcot had been careful enough to conceal the material elsewhere, for the duration of the cruise. The civil servant was certainly crafty enough for that.

"Is there a phone I can use?" he enquired, suddenly growing concerned on Mrs. Aveling's account.

"On the counter," the waiter said. "But I wouldn't be ringing there," he added, with an uneasy glance at the Ministry building and a hasty appraisal of George Mason. "It's no place for tourists. Try the railway station—the Gara—instead."

Mason smiled at the man's concern, thinking there were worlds of sympathy between ordinary human beings, no matter what ideology or system divided them. He left his coffee and disappeared inside, keeping one eye on the far side of the street in case the Rumanian emerged. With the help of the manager he dialled the American Embassy, and was put in touch immediately with the legal attaché, Everett Hodge. His message was brief and to the point:

"Your compatriot, Mrs. Walter B. Aveling, may be in some slight difficulty at the Church of St. Georghe, on the Piata 1848. She may need your assistance."

"Whom do I have the honour of addressing?" Hodge asked nervously, in a way which confirmed Mason's concern.

"George Mason," he declared, hesitating to add "Inspector" for fear of creating complications. "Care of the *Orsova* cruise."

"Much obliged to you, Mr. Mason. We'll put someone onto it right away. You did say Mrs. Aveling, didn't you?"

"That's right," Mason said, replacing the receiver with a satisfied smile, while the café owner, not comprehending a word of English, looked on indifferently.

"How much?" Mason asked, holding out a bill and pointing to the telephone and the coffee.

"5 lei," the man replied, "*mit Bedienung.*"

He handed over a bill for 6 lei and left the change, noting the name of the establishment only as he left, the Café Brasov. There seemed little point in waiting for Woolcot's contact to re-emerge into the light of day, especially as he had yet to find his way back to the Hotel Florescu. He reviewed the situation as he walked. An English civil servant makes an unscheduled stop in Budapest, then subsequently meets with agents of the Ministry of Information in Bucharest. Conclusion—he is negotiating with foreign powers for sale of classified material concealed in some mysterious manner within the covers of a conventional guidebook. An American woman, possibly a CIA agent, is interested in the same material, and is desperate enough to commit rash acts in public or jeopardise her personal safety to secure its retrieval. She is now missing, if that is the correct adjective, from the vicinity of St. Georghe's Church in Bucharest. Finally there was Herr Ziegler's interest in the same property, but his may be no more than that of an antiquarian bookseller. If not, and since there were only two sides to the Cold War, it must be assumed that Ziegler is working either with Woolcot or with Aveling. The fact that he was closely interested in the movements of the English party proved nothing either way. He was difficult to assess, and may therefore be potentially dangerous.

"Where on earth have you been, George?" Clare Dyment challenged, from her seat by the swimming pool of the Hotel Florescu. "You're late for tea."

"Took a wrong turn by the Museum," explained Mason sheepishly, as his eyes carefully searched those of Mike Woolcot, sitting nonchalantly drinking tea and conversing with Oliver Markham.

"You haven't missed much," Gayle said, deprecatingly. "Tea in these parts means exactly what it says—lemon tea with a small gateau, to tide us over until dinner."

"These tours must be costed down to the last crumb," Oliver Markham said, disgruntled. He was a big man with a correspondingly large appetite, and his eyes scanned the tray hopefully for anything left uneaten.

"Have mine," Mason said, generously, eyeing the limp cream cake without interest. "Lunch in this heat was more than enough to last me. But if there is any tea left I should . . ."

"*Is* there any left?" Clare asked mischievously, lifting the lid and peering inside what had more the appearance of a small urn than an English tea-pot. "One cup left, George. Just for you." She poured it out into the empty cup while the others, excited from their afternoon's sightseeing, looked on good-naturedly. Mason felt that he was on holiday again, from the moment he had entered the hotel garden, complete with influential Rumanians, Western tourists, lilting folk-music, the unabated afternoon sunshine.

"Had an interesting day, George?" Mike Woolcot asked. "I was almost certain you had gone off on the tour."

"George is very independent-minded," Clare explained. "He did exactly the same in Budapest and Belgrade."

A cloud seemed to pass over the civil servant's face, but he said, provocatively: "A free spirit, eh George?"

There was something about his attitude that rubbed Mason the wrong way. It may simply have been the detective's northern accent, which was still evident after six years' residence in the capital; and Mike Woolcot was one of those people to whom accent seemed to matter. If Woolcot did regard him as somehow naive and unsophisticated, that suited Mason's purpose. The more you underestimated an opponent, the more readily you dropped your guard. And there was now more than one sense in which Mason regarded the civil servant as an opponent.

"It's just that I like to see things for myself," he remarked, tentatively sipping his tea.

"Anything in particular, George?" Woolcot enquired.

Mason pondered for a moment before making his reply, thinking how cool Woolcot remained despite his dubious activities.

"I like to get the feel of a place," he said, eventually. "Something you don't get inside a bus. And I don't much care for confined spaces, the interiors of museums, churches and so on." He wondered if that remark would spur any reaction in Woolcot, but the civil servant merely glanced at Mason admiringly, as if he appreciated independence of spirit.

"We had a super time, didn't we Oliver?" Gayle remarked, with girlish enthusiasm.

"They took us right outside the city," Clare explained. "To visit a commune near the lake. There was a forest, a nature park and a beautifully-restored medieval palace."

"Rather like Venice, in some ways," Markham remarked, pedantically. "Especially the loggia facing the lake. I wanted to look it up in Bannerman, but Mike has the only copy. If I could borrow it for a minute . . ."

Woolcot smiled cunningly, withdrew the handsomely bound volume from his jacket pocket, and placed it on the table. Four separate pairs of eyes fastened to it as if it had mystical properties. Oliver Markham moved slowly to pick it up.

"Since Bannerman guides are so much sought after in these parts," Mike Woolcot said, humorously, "I am not sure I should let it out of my possession. But here, you may have it, Oliver, until dinner only." He nudged it gently towards the geography master, who picked it up and opened it ostentatiously while George Mason waited half-expectantly for something to fall out from between its pages. But no, Mike Woolcot was far too cunning for that. Besides, if Mason's theories were correct, any incriminating material had changed hands an hour ago, inside the Church of St. Georghe.

CHAPTER EIGHT

Major Peter Lang walked towards his meeting in Bolsover Gardens with considerable misgivings. The disclosures made by Lieutenant Cramer regarding his Nazi past had woken him into a bad dream, a nightmare he had long forgotten. But by a stroke of good fortune, and with the help of a colleague in Whitehall security, he had discovered at the last moment that an English friend of Cramer's, a Mr. Michael Woolcot, of Her Majesty's Diplomatic Service, was about to embark on a two-week cruise of the Danube River; and Woolcot had made no secret of the fact that the American airman had loaned him his personal copy of a well-known guidebook. There was at least a one in ten chance that was Cramer's intended method of conveying the compromising photograph to its East European destination, to finish its journey on the files of the KGB. Lang had reason to feel grateful for the efficiency of the information network he had set up in Whitehall, and for his thorough vetting of Cramer's contacts and movements over recent weeks; otherwise that tidbit of information concerning Woolcot might never have come to light. There had just been time to contact the Zurich headquarters of *Siegfried* and have their agent act quickly on his behalf.

For Alois Breitman, loyalty and duty were the strongest qualities in his training as an officer in the German Army; they had become so ingrained as to form an integral part of his soul. He was therefore uncertain how he would react in the presence of Colonel Manderson. Long years of fighting corruption, infiltration and defection in the interests of Western democracy were not lightly shed. He would dearly love to expose Cramer for the traitor he was, except that the consequences would be incalculable. There was no doubt in his mind that if the photograph reached the KGB, and it may already have done so, they would show no hesitation in using it. For the sake of his family, too, he had to preserve silence. That was the extent of his dilemma as he walked that morning to the security meeting arranged between Manderson, himself and a senior representative of Scotland Yard.

He stopped by the crossing at the end of Victoria Street and glanced at his reflection in an adjacent shop window: it returned a look of grim determination, which only too accurately reflected the dilemma confronting Alois Breitman, man of principle and of honour. It was a dilemma he would have been extremely lucky to have avoided in some form or other, during the past thirty years or so, granted the fundamental duplicity of his position. He smiled wanly at his reflection in the glass, wondering if he recognised in the highly-polished plate the face of a potential suicide. His dilemma was of those proportions; but he was also stubborn and tenacious enough to hang on, to find a way through this morass. As he gazed up doggedly at the Embassy building, he decided to play a waiting game. His own role in the pursuit of Cramer would be passive. He would leave the brunt of the work to Chief Inspector Bill Harrington, whose reputation was on a par with his own.

Forcing himself forward, he strode lightly through the main entrance and gave his name to the duty officer in the hall. After a short delay he was shown into the commanding presence of Colonel James Manderson, already in conference with the senior police officer known as Bill Harrington, a large, gruff individual, whose generous contours seemed to overflow the confines of his chair. The thin confidence he had mustered in the street began to subside as if he felt himself to be the real object of scrutiny, although on the surface they would doubtless be discussing Cramer. Bill Harrington merely nodded curtly at his entry, revealing nothing of his inner thoughts.

"I gather you two may know each other already," Manderson said, not really sure if that was the case. "However, Bill Harrington— Peter Lang."

Harrington half rose and inclined his head in deference to someone whose reputation had preceded him. Lang returned the greeting and accepted Manderson's offer of a seat, wondering uneasily what they had been talking about before his entry.

"I was discussing with Inspector Harrington," Manderson explained, as if by telepathy, "a most intriguing case—the disappearance of one of the United States' top agents in Eastern Europe, Mrs. Walter B. Aveling."

"In what circumstances?" Lang asked, at once more relaxed, but wondering what concern that would be of Harrington's.

"Her presence in Bucharest, where she was apparently assigned by the CIA, could have been alerted to the Rumanian police. But that's speculation. She was in Rumania trying to get hold of a guidebook which originated in this country, and which supposedly contained information of possible use to the other side."

"Perhaps I should explain to the major the source of my information," Harrington remarked, in view of Lang's puzzled reaction. "A junior colleague of mine, an Inspector Mason, happens at this moment—lucky chap—to be enjoying a fortnight's cruise on the Danube, from Vienna to the Black Sea. There appears to be something very unusual going on aboard that cruise which may or may not have a bearing on the fate of Mrs. Aveling. Mason, however, mentions nothing of a woman agent: he may not recognise one if he saw her. He was anxious to report the suspicious behaviour of a fellow tourist, a Swiss by the name of Anton Ziegler, whom he has asked me to investigate. I approached the Swiss branch of Interpol, who confirmed that Ziegler operates an antiquarian bookshop in Zurich, on the Neumarkt. Apparently, the same address is known to them as the headquarters of an organisation called *Siegfried*."

"*Siegfried*?" Lang enquired, in mock-innocence. "What on earth is that?"

"Something of a left-over from the war," Harrington explained. "Practically defunct, since the vast majority of its beneficiaries will be either dead or retired."

"Could you explain yourself?" Lang requested.

"*Siegfried*," continued Harrington, "is an organisation whose sole purpose is to protect former Nazis, place them in safe employment, for example, and guard them from arrest. They have influence in some very high places."

"I fail to understand, Inspector," Lang countered, "what possible connection this Herr Ziegler could have with an agent of the CIA."

"If Mason has got his facts straight," Harrington put in, as ever sceptical about his subordinate's competence, "it won't be the first time he has led everyone off on a wild goose chase. I remember a case in . . ."

"Didn't you say, Chief Inspector," Manderson interrupted, "that the book in question, *Bannerman's Guide*, was taken on board the *Orsova* by a traveller from this country? Major Lang, there are five British tourists on board that boat, one of whom is Bill Harrington's colleague, George Mason. That leaves the other four as possible traitors: a geography teacher from Slough, a typist from Stepney, and—interestingly enough—a junior official at the Foreign Office, called Michael Woolcot. There is a second woman, Clare Dyment, who apparently works in Woolcot's department."

Lang permitted himself a smile for the first time since entering the beautifully furnished second-floor office, which overlooked the square and lower Pimlico.

"The answer is obvious," he exclaimed, enthusiastically. "Your Foreign Office personnel! They would be the ones with the contacts and the motives. Their line of country." At the same time, he realised at once that his hunch regarding Cramer's methods was correct, and that the object of CIA interest was the very photograph Ziegler was trying to retrieve on his behalf. Could the CIA already suspect that, in protecting Cramer, he was also shielding S? It was an uncomfortable thought.

"Now hold on a minute, Major Lang," Harrington cautioned. "Aren't you making a rather large-sized assumption there?"

"Seems obvious to me," the ex-Nazi persisted.

"At least three of the passengers were carrying almost identical copies of the same book!" Harrington exclaimed, with a glance towards Manderson that gave Lang the sinking, paranoiac feeling that they knew something which concerned himself. He was almost tempted to make a clean breast of things, but he pursed his lips and held on.

"That does rather complicate matters," he agreed, in his impeccable English idiom. "Then it could be any one of them."

"Exactly," Harrington said. "They are all equally suspect; yet at the same time they could all be perfectly innocent. The material contained in the book could have been planted there without the bearer's knowledge."

Obviously they knew less than he did. They did not know that Cramer had loaned the guide to Woolcot. They would have known nothing but for the bungling interference of George Mason. What a hundred-to-one chance that a member of Harrington's own staff would be on board!

"Exactly. And since there turned out to be more than one copy of the book, that would become an increasingly complicated and uncertain procedure," Harrington went on, "involving Mrs. Aveling in a great deal of time and effort. She was tired and due for a holiday, and she expected to have the whole business sewn up in Budapest. Instead of which, she was last reported operating in Rumania."

"There we have the makings of a mystery," Lang said, now nursing the quiet conviction that, with the CIA out of the running, Herr Ziegler would have no great difficulty retrieving the evidence. Near-defunct *Siegfried* might be, but it had always employed extremely able people.

"Mason is the one on the spot," Harrington said. "We shall have to rely on him to keep us abreast of the latest developments."

"Are you just going to sit back and wait?" the Colonel enquired, in surprise. "You could invite Major Lang here to do some preliminary checking up on the two Foreign Office personnel, as the likeliest avenue of enquiry. With the utmost discretion, of course, since we may be dealing with two entirely innocent and conscientious individuals."

Harrington glanced expectantly at the Major, who was beginning to feel increasingly reassured. The more aspects of this interesting case he could keep under his personal control, the greater the chance he had of saving his own skin; added to that would be the knowledge that he was acting in the interests of his adoptive country. For his own self-respect, Major Peter Lang, alias Alois Breitman, required such an assurance.

"You must think me unpardonably rude, Major," Harrington suddenly remarked. "For inviting you here to talk about one thing, and going on all the while about something quite different."

"Ah, yes," echoed Colonel Manderson. "Now to the business of the airman, Lieutenant Cramer . . . ."

CHAPTER NINE

The question which exercised George Mason's mind, as the *Orsova* steamed through the agricultural plains of eastern Rumania on its approach to the Danube delta, was the exact nature of the information which had changed hands in the church in Bucharest. Of one thing he was certain: it was information enough to engage the interest of both the CIA, in the person of Mrs. Walter B. Aveling, and the Rumanian Ministry of Information. He wondered too if Ziegler's interest was more than a professional one, since the bookseller always seemed near at hand whenever there had been an incident, on every occasion except the most recent, in Bucharest. He was waiting for Harrington's reply to his telegram, and had given the Eforie Hotel in Mammaia, their last port of call on the Danube trip, as a forwarding address.

After an appetising lunch of river fish and *soupe paysanne*, Oliver and Gayle retreated from the heat for a game of chess in the forward lounge, mainly he thought as a pretext for being alone together. Clare went resolutely up on deck determined to add to a nicely maturing sun-tan. He sought her out, not merely for the pleasure of her company, but also to question her about Mike Woolcot, to find out as much as he could about his activities and contacts in London.

"It's a funny thing about those books," he remarked, drawing up a chair in full view of her long brown limbs, which she stretched out across the deck.

Clare glanced at him, from behind tinted glasses. It was difficult to tell if her expression was one of interest, boredom or indifference.

"I thought that was all over and done with, George," she said, languidly. "Enjoy your lunch?"

"Excellent," he replied. "Nothing like fresh river fish; especially in heat like this, if you can't work up much of an appetite."

"It's all the sitting around we do," she said, letting her fingers trail lightly across the deck, between the two chairs. His arm dangled, so that his fingers touched and interlocked with hers. It was part of an innocent holiday flirtation of which she approved; and she enjoyed being the focus of rivalry between two very different men.

The time had arrived, Mason considered, to take her fully into his confidence, on the assumption that her sense of patriotism would outweigh her loyalty to a professional colleague. If she were not trustworthy, then no one was on this entire bizarre cruise, not even the staid Oliver Markham, who had been assiduously keeping a personal log of the voyage since leaving Vienna, to present with slides to the Slough Geographic Society.

He tightened his grip on the slender fingers entwined with his own, as if for reassurance and said:

"There is something I wanted to tell you."

The girl reacted in slight alarm, removing her sunglasses and looking him steadily in the face, perhaps expecting a declaration of passion, induced by the splendid meal, the sunshine, the romantic atmosphere.

"Go on," she jolted, since he stalled.

"About my job," he said. "I never mentioned what it was . . ."

"Is that all?" she cried, sinking back into the deck-chair with a mixture of relief and disappointment. "I know that already. You're a policeman."

Mason's eyes opened wide in incredulity.

"How on earth did you . . . ?" he stuttered.

"Easy," she said, laughing. "You gave it away in your questioning of Mike. As if you really suspected him of something."

Mason cleared his throat. It was as well that she had guessed and did not seem to mind. People's feelings about policemen were unpredictable.

"About the guidebooks," he began again, now that the first hurdle was cleared.

"Playing detective games again, George?" she jibed. "Or is this for real?"

"This is deadly serious," he said.

The girl swung round facing him, freeing her arm and folding it in the other, in a gesture of impatience.

"This whole series of incidents: Mike's misadventure in Budapest, the loss of your guidebook in Belgrade, and there was something else which happened in Rumania, that I haven't mentioned to anyone."

"In Bucharest?" she asked, growing more intent from the look of earnestness on his face.

"All these separate incidents are really connected," he went on. "When you all went off to Lake Moga..."

"Mogosoaia?"

"They have such difficult words, in this country. I was even struggling with the street names in Bucharest."

"Rumanian is a Romance language," Clare sympathetically explained. "It's related to Italian, or even French."

"You could have fooled me!"

"Now you're side-tracking, George," she chided. "What happened while we were on the guided tour?"

"How well do you know Mike Woolcot?" he asked, obliquely.

"Well enough," she replied lightly. "We work together, we go out together sometimes, we have friends in common. But we do not feel tied."

Mason was relieved to hear it on account of his theories on Woolcot. Yet he had never seriously imagined they were romantically involved.

"What sort of friends does he keep outside of working hours?"

"Come off it, George!" she said, suddenly reading his mind. "What is all this leading up to? You're surely not seriously suggesting that poor old Woolly..."

"Is that what you call him?" Mason asked, in amusement.

The girl flashed dark eyes at him, mercilessly.

"You surely don't hold Mike responsible for all this mysteriousness about books, secret towers, and so on. The whole idea is preposterous. Wasn't he questioned by the Hungarian police?"

"You did not answer my question," he said, sipping his beer.

"About his friends in London? I only knew the ones we had in common. He knows lots of people. You should ask him."

"Do you happen to know who loaned him the Bannerman? Another colleague, perhaps? Or just a friend?"

"He may have mentioned it, but I don't recall. I merely assumed it was his own copy, and I wanted one like it. I could ask him if you like."

Mason was cautious. "If you do that now," he said, "it would only arouse his suspicions."

The girl looked furiously back at him, her eyes blazing with hostility. "Won't you please tell me what you're driving at?"

"There will be plenty of time for explanations later," he said. "If you tip off Woolcot, or Woolly if you prefer, you might place me in a very delicate, not to say dangerous, position."

The girl glanced at him curiously, simmered and gradually relaxed, but she did not speak for several moments. Instead, she sipped her drink and gazed out over the ship's rail at the passing scenery. Mason's eye took in the smooth brown curves of her body. Women were always more beautiful when they were angry.

"I shall only trust you," she remarked, with the beginnings of compliance, "if you tell me everything you know or suspect."

Mason swallowed hard. Sooner or later, no doubt, he would have to trust somebody. He might as well start with Clare.

"I am looking for some kind of thread," he began, "that joins these incidents together. Let us suppose, as a working hypothesis, that Mike Woolcot was not really arrested in Budapest—that story about the Kossuth Tower never wholly convinced me, in any case. Suppose instead that he was carrying classified information from London to a contact in Eastern Europe."

The girl's eyes opened wide in amazement, but she did not interrupt.

"The information, whatever it is, did not change hands in Budapest, for reasons we may be able to explain later. But he may very well have been briefed there on who his contact should be, how he should meet him and so forth."

"For a policeman," Clare said coldly, "you have a vivid imagination."

"The CIA are also interested in the same material, but they do not know which of the three copies is the relevant one. That would explain Mrs. Aveling's unusual behaviour in the Hotel Vlad, as well as the theft of your copy in Belgrade."

"Which side was the thief on?" she asked, growing visibly more interested at the mention of Belgrade.

"Impossible to say," Mason explained. "On the face of it, he could have been working for either side. What is certain is that Mrs. Aveling had Woolcot marked by the time we reached Bucharest."

"How do you know that?" Clare asked, considerably impressed.

"Because she never took her eyes off him from the moment he left the Hotel Florescu until he reached the Piata 1848 and the Church of St. Georghe."

"What happened then?" she asked, intensely curious.

"Woolcot met a Rumanian national, whom I later followed back to the Ministry of Information. I did not see Mrs. Aveling at any time inside the church. I can only assume that she in turn was under surveillance, and was possibly arrested by the secret police. I am almost certain information changed hands inside the church."

"Do you mind if I have another drink?" Clare asked, "to wash all that down?"

"Same again?" he asked, calling the deck waiter.

"All this is quite fascinating," the girl agreed. "And the facts do need an explanation. But aren't you overlooking two rather important matters?"

"Am I?" he asked in some surprise, but willing to stand correction.

"In the first place," she said, "if Mike's copy of the book was so charged with secret information, he would scarcely have let it out of his sight for one moment. Instead of which, he lent it to all sorts of people, including yourself."

Mason knit his brows. She certainly had a point there. The civil servant, in the light of his theories, had been careless to the point of recklessness.

"Confidence," Mason declared, giving it some thought. "He is so supremely confident of himself that he could afford to lend the book to anyone who asked for it, to avoid arousing suspicion. He would hardly expect a contingent of the Special Branch on board a Danube cruise."

"What about motive?" she continued. "If you are implying that he is a traitor, which sounds fantastic to me, even after what you described in Bucharest, he would need some sort of motive. I have never known him to be anything but completely devoted to the service and to his country."

Mason could see that he would never shake her conviction.

"Just assure me of one thing," Mason pleaded. "Your absolute discretion. If he ever . . ."

"I am not sure I believe in all your theories," she replied, compliantly. "But I do understand that you have a job to do. You can count on my absolute discretion."

Mason smiled and felt more relaxed. He sipped his beer and gazed out over the ship's rail. Cruises were not a wholly satisfactory experience, he reflected: days of endless lethargy, between spates of frantic sight-seeing and activity. And this cruise had seen more than enough of the latter. There was old Ziegler playing deck chess with one of his compatriots, every so often lifting his eyes in the direction of Clare Dyment and himself. What part did he play in all this? And when would Harrington write?

"I thought you might help me over the motive," he said, after a while. "Just something to go off, more or less."

"Mike never discussed his politics with me," she said. "As civil servants we are supposed to be neutral."

"Is he happy at work?" Mason asked. In his experience, acts of treachery were often committed out of a sense of grudge, arising from some real or imagined injustice. Like the sacked employee setting fire to the work's premises; or the cashier putting his hand in the till.

The girl thought for a long time. He began to feel that she was coming over to his view of things, and would help him if she could, even if only partially convinced.

"Nothing springs to mind," she said, eventually. "Mike has always seemed quite satisfied at work, with his job, the people he works with . . ."

"What about promotion?"

"He put in for a transfer eighteen months ago, to the Paris office. They had a vacancy for Third Secretary."

"He didn't get it?"

Clare shook her head thoughtfully. "The post went to an Oxford man, who was already in France and spoke French fluently. Mike has always had some difficulty with the language side of the work. And besides, he's not a graduate. Came up the hard way, straight from school."

"Isn't that a disadvantage, in your line of work?"

"Mike knows as well as I do that university graduates get quicker promotion. It's only natural. He's come a long way already, with his background. Perhaps he sees further advancement blocked, I don't know. At least he never complained to me about it."

"All the same," Mason thought, "it's an interesting speculation. *Something* must have changed his loyalties."

"You said it, not me," the girl replied, tartly.

The scenery became distinctly less spectacular, now that the mountains and gorges were a long way behind them. The Danube had broadened considerably, and was filled with ocean-going ships that dwarfed the modest *Orsova* plying midstream, far from the banks and the rolling countryside beyond. They were suspended between two states, the river forming the boundary between them. A kind of no man's land, between Bulgaria and Rumania. It remained that way for the whole of that day and part of the next, until they disembarked at Hirsova for the coach to Mammaia, which they reached late in the afternoon.

On arrival at the Eforie Hotel, George Mason did not join the others bathing in the private swimming pool, for the simple reason that he had forgotten to pack his swimming trunks. He took a walk instead, along the straight and uneventful promenade of Mammaia, with its magnificent flower beds on the one hand, the gleaming silver sand and the tranquil breakers on the other. To his mind, it was indistinguishable from scores of similar resorts, replete with speedily-built, impersonal hotels, all along the Mediterranean coastline. But it was a bather's paradise, a sailor's paradise and, if his guidebook was accurate, the right place to come for mud-baths in Lake Siutghiol which, together with the sea, hemmed the resort into one long narrow isthmus of land between Constanta and Cape Midia to the north.

By the time he had returned to the hotel and taken a shower it was almost time for dinner. He dressed carefully and went down to the bar for a quick drink, watching the lights through the hotel windows illumining the surf on the beach below. It grew dark quite early, but he could still make out the shadows of tourists coming up the sand from an evening bathe, wondering if Clare and the others had been among them.

Suddenly, however, she was at his elbow, with a rather worried-looking Gayle Sumner beside her.

"Don't suppose Oliver has come down yet?" she enquired, glancing anxiously around her and through the open doors leading into the dining-room.

"Nope," replied Mason, nonchalantly. He felt quite tired after a long walk, and this was one evening he was not going to play the detective.

"Do you suppose he came up from the beach?" Clare said. "He may have forgotten the time."

"Beach?" asked Mason, in surprise. "I thought you all went to the pool."

"We did," Gayle replied, "at first. But Oliver thought the sea would be more bracing. He took off to the beach with Anton Ziegler about an hour ago."

"While you both stayed up here with Mike?"

Gayle nodded.

Mason thought for a long moment, gazing out at the dark mass of water beyond the stretch of silver sand.

"I don't suppose you happened to notice," he remarked after a while, "whether he still had Mike's guidebook with him?"

"I'm almost sure he did," Clare Dyment said. "It was in the pocket of his beach-robe."

"That might explain a lot," Mason said, ordering a round of drinks, while Clare and Gayle looked curiously at him, not sure exactly what he meant.

"Here comes old Ziegler now," Mason remarked, as the Swiss entered the room followed by two men, one in a plain suit, the other in dark uniform.

"With what looks very much like . . ." Clare said, uneasily.

". . . the local police?"

"And they're heading this way," Gayle said, swallowing hard.

PART TWO

UPSTREAM

CHAPTER TEN

It was a dispirited English party that set off back to the waiting *Orsova* early the following morning. Oliver Markham's body had been transferred to the local morgue after he had been found drowned on the foreshore. Police questioning had taken up most of the previous evening and they had seemed satisfied, perhaps too easily satisfied, with Herr Ziegler's report that the teacher had gone too far out and got into difficulties, while he had returned to the hotel to get help. Ziegler had undergone the longest interrogation, but as the two of them had been alone together there was no one to challenge or verify his story; and the police, called out late-evening, were in no mood to create difficulties. Arrangements would be made, they conceded, to have the body flown back to England if Oliver's family requested it. Their verdict: accidental death by drowning, which was by no means an uncommon occurrence along this stretch of the Rumanian coast.

Gayle Sumner, too distressed by the tragedy to continue her holiday, booked the next flight back from Mammaia, so that she could convey the news personally to Oliver's parents, living retired in Hampshire.

Mason was in two minds about the incident, ever mindful of Harrington's exhortation to keep his nose clean and avoid complications. The Bannerman, of course, was missing; which fact alone pointed an accusing finger at the elderly Swiss. Yet it seemed hardly credible that someone as apparently frail as Ziegler could help bring about the death by drowning of a much stronger and younger man; unless of course he had special training. More plausible was the possibility that Oliver had got into difficulties,

misjudging depths and tides in unfamiliar water; and that Ziegler
had taken advantage of his plight to seize the commodity he most
prized: Woolcot's guide. In any event, it had been a shattering
note on which to end the first leg of their cruise, and an ill omen
for the start of their return. Mason would need to keep a close eye
on both Woolcot and Ziegler; with only the half-convinced Clare
Dyment for moral support. And Harrington's telegram, which he
was supposed to pick up at the Eforie, had somehow not arrived.
He would have to wire him a new forwarding address for the trip
back.

When they reached the boat, Mason found that dinner had
been put back to one hour after sailing. Anton Ziegler was drinking
alone in the bar, the Bannerman guide resting innocently beside
his glass.

"Good evening, Herr Mason," Ziegler said, as he entered.

Mason muttered something in reply. It was the first occasion
they had spoken together in the course of the last seven days.
Now was as good a time as any to get acquainted.

"May I offer you a drink?"

"Beer," Mason said. "Export."

"Unfortunate about your friend, Mr. Markham," he remarked,
guardedly, as if to test the other's reaction.

"Very unfortunate," Mason said, looking Ziegler straight in
the eye. "In fact it has just about ruined the holiday for all of us."

"Can't understand what made him go so far out," the Swiss
said. "He was obviously not a very good swimmer."

"Obviously," Mason said, with heavy emphasis.

"I feel as if I were somehow to blame, Mr. Mason. I should
have checked his . . . enthusiasm."

"But you didn't."

The Swiss coughed in embarrassment. "I must admit I kept
close in to the shore. My doctor has advised me against strenuous
exercise."

It began to sound to Mason that Oliver had in fact engineered
his own death. If it were not for Ziegler's obvious interest in the
book . . . but the local police had closed the incident and there
was no way now that Ziegler's innocence could be officially
questioned.

"Finished with the book?" he asked.

Ziegler's gaze did not falter. "I brought it up to give back to Mr. Woolcot. Should have thought of it earlier, but in all the upset, you understand . . ."

"You found it on the beach, with Oliver's things?"

"I suppose I should have handed it to the police last night, but since it was not strictly Mr. Markham's property . . ."

"Very thoughtful of you, I am sure," Mason said, as pointedly as he could. "Is it really a valuable collector's piece? I should have thought there would be other copies in equally good condition."

A curious look appeared in Ziegler's eyes, from which it appeared he was trying to decide if Mason really knew something, or if he were merely fishing. He seemed to decide the latter, if only for comfort's sake, and absorbed his attention in his drink.

"Another beer, Herr Mason, before dinner?"

"Allow me," the detective said, reaching in his pocket. "Same again?"

Ziegler nodded, deliberatively. "Quite a good beer," he said. "Not the equal of a German pilsner, perhaps, but comparable in some respects." He held his glass up to the light, to examine it.

"A pint of bitter would suit me," Mason thought, but he did not express it. Comparisons in beverage seemed irrelevant at this point. Ziegler's shiftiness was not.

"I met an acquaintance of yours," he said, becoming even more direct. "A Mrs. Aveling, in Belgrade. She also seemed interested in the book, but it was the wrong edition."

Ziegler's eyes grew larger. Raising his glass to his lips, he drank for a moment before making his reply.

"Mrs. who?" he asked.

"Mrs. Walter B. Aveling. An American saleswoman of some kind."

"I am afraid you have the advantage of me," he said. "I know very few Americans. None of them answers to that name."

"Then I must be mistaken," Mason said, sheepishly, drawing the obvious conclusion that Ziegler and Aveling were not working in collusion.

Perhaps it was only of academic interest at this point, since whatever the book had contained had almost certainly changed hands inside the Church of St. Georghe, Bucharest. But he was beginning to wonder exactly who Ziegler was working for. He had

Woolcot linked with the KGB, Aveling with the CIA. Or was Ziegler's denial merely a form of professional discretion and he knew the American woman after all? What was certain was that the devious Swiss book collector was going to volunteer as little as possible. Mason would have to uncover everything for himself, even if that meant placing himself in physical danger. One death already, either accidental or planned, was sufficient proof of that.

"I must confess, Mr. Mason," Ziegler said, picking up the book and fondling it, "that I was at one stage extremely interested in Mr. Woolcot's book. You know, I actually made him a very handsome offer for it, but he rejected it out of hand. Said it was not his to sell. Now if I could discover the actual owner of the book I might still make a bid for it—for its antiquarian value, you understand. But not so much as I originally had in mind."

Mason smiled enigmatically and sipped his drink. "Which settles one point, at least," he thought to himself. "The KGB have beaten you to it!"

At that point, Clare Dyment and Mike Woolcot entered the bar, but from the look on their faces Mason could tell that it was going to be a very subdued dinner party that night.

One day out, after a sudden squall which caused the boat to pitch and roll, and the depleted English party to retreat to their bunks, the *Orsova* again called at Giurgiu for the transfer to Bucharest. The Foreign Office pair boarded together, confirming what had already been apparent to Mason since they had left the Black Sea: they were still firm friends, and whatever the girl had made of his confidential disclosures, it had not in the least affected her attitude towards Woolcot. There was something else which struck Mason as unusual, but in the light of his theories it was readily explained. Not since Budapest, eight days and many hundred miles ago, had the young diplomat signed up for the guided tour organised by Intourist. Now he was more than eager to take part, prompted by Clare's enthusiasm for the environs of Lake Mogosoaia. That seemed to indicate that his previous business in the Rumanian capital was complete. Mason switched his attention to Anton Ziegler.

Contrary to form, the Swiss did not leave with the others on the coach which drew up after lunch outside the Hotel Florescu, but commenced walking instead along the Calea Victoriei, one of the main streets. Mason also excused himself, curious to find out what sort of company, if any, the Swiss would keep on his afternoon off, or whether he would confine his activities to visiting secondhand bookshops. Mason also had in mind, time permitting, a quick visit to the American Embassy, to see if they had news of Mrs. Aveling. He had never quite got over her disappearance from the church.

Ziegler walked unhurriedly down the entire length of the broad boulevard, keeping beneath the shade of the overhanging trees. His first stop was at a bookshop. He glanced in the window for a few moments, then disappeared inside, re-emerging fifteen minutes later carrying a small package under his arm. An addition to his collection, Mason thought, beginning to enjoy his casual eavesdropping on the unsuspecting Swiss. It was more interesting than visiting churches, monuments and the dark interiors of museums; and there was Ziegler's proximity to Oliver Markham on the day he had drowned. Mason would never accept as final the Swiss's version of that incident, which meant that, from now on any independent movements on his part would need careful vetting.

If Mason hoped, however, that Ziegler's afternoon stroll would help unravel the mystery of the guidebooks, he was soon disappointed. The Swiss soon became totally absorbed in the open-air book market at the end of the *calea* and Mason was loathe to spend the remainder of the afternoon dodging from stall to stall in what seemed the unlikely expectation that Ziegler would betray anything more than a wholly professional interest in old books. His interest had also waned in Woolcot's guide; but that could be because he had not found in it what he had expected to find when he had picked it up from among Oliver's pile of clothes lying on the beach. On Mason's reading of things, Mike Woolcot had long since removed any sensitive material concealed within it. During what remained of the couple of hours before the tour bus returned to the Hotel Florescu, he decided to pay a call at the American Embassy on Dionisei Lupu Street, to find out as much as he could about the vanishing American, Mrs. Walter B. Aveling; and also to see if he could not get some clues as to what this wild goose chase about *Bannerman's Guide* was all about.

The legal attaché, Mr. Everett Hodge, received him amicably in his office at the rear of the building, beneath the revolving electric fan, the Venetian blind lowered to filter the brilliant sunlight.

"You said your name was . . . ?" he enquired, uncorking a fresh bottle of Scotch.

"Mason," the detective said. "Inspector Mason, from London."

"A policeman, eh?" Hodge said. "Don't get many visitors from the old country. Though we are a bit off the beaten track."

"In a manner of speaking," Mason explained, slightly overawed by the expansive American diplomat, "we have met before. I telephoned you three days ago."

The American suddenly recalled.

"About Mrs. Aveling?" he asked. "I remember you expressed certain fears for her safety."

"I thought at the time," Mason declared, "and I still think, that she was abducted from the Church of St. Georghe. I saw her enter, but she did not come back out. There has been no sign of her since."

"So you telephoned us? Very thoughtful of you, Mr. Mason. I appreciate it." But the diplomat was inclined to be dismissive. He went on: "You need have no cause for concern on Mrs. Aveling's behalf. She is one of our most experienced agents and knows very well how to handle herself."

"You don't think she is in any trouble?" Mason said, in surprise.

"If she was I am sure the Rumanian authorities would have notified us before this. They are usually very quick to advertise their little victories, shall we say, in the game of espionage. I have no good reason to believe that Mrs. Aveling is not free and well and up to her ears in work."

"May I have another scotch?" Mason asked.

"Help yourself," Hodge said, pushing the tray towards Mason, at the same time watching him curiously. He was going to ask him for official identity, but Mason had not brought papers on the cruise. His best chance lay in keeping the initiative.

"Have you any idea why Mrs. Aveling was interested in a copy of *Bannerman's Guide?*" he asked.

"Only because she kept on about it all the way down the Danube River. Bumped into her practically everywhere we stopped."

Hodge smiled opaquely, leant back and carefully lit a cigar.

"Tell me more," he prompted. "Since you evidently know something."

"It is my belief," Mason said, "that the guidebook contained classified information of some kind. Perhaps you have some idea what it was."

Hodge stalled for a few moments, as if wondering how far he could trust his visitor; during which time the room filled with heavy cigar smoke.

"Mrs. Aveling was acting on a tip-off," he said, eventually overcoming his doubts, "from someone on the staff of our embassy in London."

"A tip-off?" Mason asked, in puzzlement.

"The story as I have it from reliable sources is as follows," Hodge said. "A former German officer, who did not give his name, rang the embassy and explained that he had given to Lieutenant Robert Cramer evidence linking a senior member of MI5 with the German SS."

"But why would he contact the Americans and not the British Special Branch?"

"I've thought a lot about that," Hodge admitted, "and the only conclusion I can come to is that the informant wanted to make sure we knew Cramer had that evidence."

"So you could make sure he did not keep it to himself?"

"Exactly, Inspector. He wanted to make sure Cramer used the evidence."

"But so far he hasn't?"

Hodge shook his head. "For some reason best known to himself, Cramer is sitting on that document."

"Shielding someone?"

"That would seem the obvious conclusion," Hodge agreed, "but there is a little more to it than that."

"Go on," Mason urged, growing more attentive at every moment.

Hodge cleared his throat and poured himself another drink, while the revolving fan ticked ominously in the heat.

"Perhaps unknown to his original German contact, but known well enough to our own security services, Lieutenant Cramer came under suspicion some time ago over the question of access to classified information kept by defence personnel. There was never sufficient evidence to confront him openly with any charges and the matter was dropped. Cramer was simply transferred to a less-sensitive department."

"So?" Mason said, anxiously checking his watch.

"The question against his name remained," said Hodge. "And added to it is the information the nameless German gave to him. Don't you see, Inspector? The case against him is wide open again."

"You think he slipped it inside the guidebook and sent it on a long voyage eastwards, courtesy of the *Orsova?*"

"That may not be so fantastic as it sounds," Hodge explained. "We know, for example, that he took the initiative in contacting a young British diplomat, Mike Woolcot, whom he scarcely knew, and pressed the guidebook on him."

"But how did he become aware of Woolcot's holiday plans, if he hardly knew him?"

"I think they had a girl-friend in common, who must have mentioned it to him."

"Don't tell me her name," Mason said. "I know it already."

"Clare . . . ?"

". . . Dyment!"

"But how . . . ?"

"She is also in the cruise party," Mason said, with an uneasy smile.

CHAPTER ELEVEN

M ajor Lang was not very helpful when Chief Inspector Harrington called on him for news of developments on what had come to be known as "The American Case"; he resented the constant intrusion from Scotland Yard, which made him feel increasingly insecure, as if they were watching him. He was determined to soft-pedal and to keep any hard facts he obtained to himself. The question of his own survival had now superseded all other considerations. Spies were arrested frequently enough; others defected. Why should he, Peter Lang, risk exposure, loss of office, and the fruits of a long and dedicated career for the sake of a traitor on the staff of the American Embassy?

"I have been keeping close tabs on Cramer," he explained, in an attempt to placate the detective. "So far he has kept his nose clean."

Harrington grumbled noisily.

"Hasn't he contacted anyone from the other side?" he enquired.

Lang shook his head, looking Harrington straight in the eye to avoid any suggestion of lying. He was aware that Cramer was just now out of the country—Manderson had told him as much the other day—but he did not know precisely where, apart from a cryptic reference to Munich.

"Personally, I think it's a false lead," he said. "You know how nervous some people get over security leaks. Yet they happen all the time."

Harrington grinned, but he was both disappointed and puzzled. Mason was definitely on to something, which had begun right here in London. He had never mentioned a Robert Cramer, presumably because he had nothing on him; but in Harrington's mind the two seemed to connect. "Wasn't there something about a bookshop in Wessex Square?" he asked.

Lang slowly nodded, feeling an inner panic. Evans had evidently mentioned their visit, and it was up to him to explain it away. "We thought there *might* be a connection," he said. "We followed him there on several occasions, but when we moved in the airman was clean—no incriminating evidence of any kind."

"How do you account for his frequent visits?"

The former German officer merely shrugged, as if it were of little importance. "Perhaps he has a genuine interest in old books."

Harrington smiled and appeared at least partially satisfied.

"You haven't given up on him, have you?" he asked.

"If he is involved in any kind of espionage activity," Lang explained, "which on the face of things does not appear very likely, then he will have to make his contact somewhere, somehow, in or around the city of London. When that time comes, Inspector . . ."

Harrington looked for a long curious moment at his counterpart. For a man of his daunting reputation Lang appeared to be playing the "American Case" very low key. A thought crossed his mind but he dismissed it. Lang's background was unimpeachable. Harrington was a man who respected status, reputation and everything that went with it—to his mind, truthfulness, reliability, honesty. All the same the nagging thought persisted that Lang might be holding something back.

"Any news of Woolcot then?" he asked, more optimistically. "Inspector Mason has named him as a strong suspect, whether or not this Cramer is involved."

Lang was more reassuring on that point.

"I can say quite definitely that the two men were acquainted," he replied, "even if we have no grounds for linking them in an espionage chain. The American is an habitual socialiser, well-known at embassy receptions."

"Mason was emphatic that Woolcot has been handling classified information," Harrington said. "According to him, the material has already changed hands, inside a church in Bucharest."

Lang gave a cynical smile, as if to say: the bird has flown, what need is there for us to involve ourselves more? Just to pull some chestnuts out of the fire for the American State Department? At the same time his hopes sank that *Siegfried* might retrieve the photograph first.

Harrington caught the drift of the other's look, and he for one was not a man to engage either himself or his staff—to wit, Inspector Mason—in needless expense of time and energy. Except that the involvement of Michael Woolcot would bring the problem right home to roost here in the British Foreign Office.

"We must try and nail this chap Woolcot, at the very least," he explained. "Whether the goods have gone overboard or not." The major nodded in sympathy. Cramer was one kettle of fish, Woolcot another.

"There is a motive," he said, suggestively. "Woolcot was turned down for promotion two years ago. His superiors confided to me that his lack of a university background would prevent him rising much higher in the Service. He has apparently been champing at the bit for the best part of two years now. That does not mean that they doubt his loyalty."

"Did you give them a reason to do so?" Harrington asked.

"What do you think?" the other said. "We need a good deal more to go off than Mason's suspicions. After all, he may simply have been trading in obscene photographs."

"Photographs?" asked Harrington, with alacrity. "Who said anything about photographs?"

"Merely a manner of speaking," Lang said, hastily covering his mistake.

Along the sun-drenched pavements of Dunavska Street, George Mason set the moored *Orsova* determinedly behind him and hurried towards the British Embassy. Of the members of the English party, only Clare Dyment took off on the guided tour. Mike Woolcot made vague references to the Budapest Ethnographical Museum and the Academy of Fine Arts, which he had missed on his previous visit, while Ziegler was going to visit the second-hand bookshops in the University precinct. Mason could have followed either one of them, but what he stood most in need of now were firm facts to substantiate what Everett Hodge had told him at the American Embassy. As he went he was keenly conscious of his isolation; not even Clare Dyment, as personal friend of Robert Cramer, was above suspicion, for she had apparently introduced the American to Mike Woolcot. The intriguing question was whether she was more than a personal friend.

Grayson, the Second Secretary, recalled his previous visit and at once asked news of Woolcot, who was still missing when they had first met. He felt concern, not only for the fate of a British tourist, but for a junior member of the diplomatic corps.

Mason accepted his offer of a drink and sank back into the cool upholstery of a leather armchair. He was a large man, unaccustomed to the heat, and the hurried walk had tired him.

"It was about Mr. Woolcot that I called again," he said, when he had regained his breath.

"He is still missing?" Grayson asked, in alarm.

"On the contrary," Mason replied, "he is very much in evidence. Certain of his activities have given cause for grave concern."

"Could you explain that, Inspector?"

The detective cleared his throat and said: "Woolcot claimed that he had been arrested for trespass in Budapest, and that his camera was confiscated. He was eventually released and rejoined the *Orsova* minutes before she left Belgrade. Since then he has been in touch, to my almost certain knowledge, with an agent of the Rumanian Secret Service."

"You can't be serious, Mr. Mason!" Grayson protested. "How can you possibly think that?"

Mason told him the story as he knew it, and also of the American interest in the same material, and Mrs. Aveling's strange disappearance. He then went on to describe the circumstances of Oliver's death and his suspicions of Anton Ziegler.

"You are on very delicate ground here," Grayson cautioned. "The material you describe obviously means a lot to three very different parties. You could be placing youself in a position of grave personal danger, and even if you are right about Woolcot, there is very little you can do about it in your present position. You will have to wait until you return to London."

"What would you advise?" asked Mason.

"Keep a low profile and enjoy what remains of your cruise. Continue amassing any evidence that comes your way, in the form of contacts, suspicious behaviour and so on. You will then have a fairly large dossier to present to your superiors in London. They will decide what action to take."

That seemed sensible advice, and Mason agreed to adopt it. There would be nothing Grayson nor anyone else could do for him if he made a false move; and Harrington certainly wouldn't thank him for it.

"I was expecting something from London," he said, finally. "I used your embassy as a forwarding address."

"Wait one moment, while I check in the outer office."

When he left the room, the detective's eye surveyed the large, comfortably furnished office lined with bookshelves, filing cabinets and photographs of the Lune Valley. A fly fisherman, perhaps; or maybe Grayson was born there and felt homesick for that quiet, overlooked part of England. The way Mason did, sometimes, for the Yorkshire Dales.

The secretary returned with a smile of satisfaction and handed over a sealed envelope which Mason eagerly tore open.

"What you were expecting?" he asked.

"It's from Harrington all right," the detective explained. "But it confirms nothing either way. He merely states that they have nothing so far on Woolcot, but investigations are proceeding. Ziegler, on the other hand, may be working for an organisation known as *Siegfried*, which exists to help and protect ex-Nazis. What do you make of that?

Grayson's surprise was as great as Mason's.

"I should have thought an organisation like that would have wrapped up long ago," he said.

"Apparently not," replied Mason, "if Ziegler is anything to go by." He was now on a spot, and he knew it. Harrington would be expecting some kind of concrete result from all this. But how?

"I wish you well," Grayson said, with a look that betrayed both anxiety and sympathy. "And bon voyage!"

Once outside the building he turned sharply into Franzuska Street, and had not walked very far when he spotted two familiar figures a short way ahead of him. It was Woolcot and his Rumanian contact strolling unhurriedly from the Ethnographical Museum. The Rumanian was unmistakable, since Mason had seen him quite clearly from a distance of a few feet in the Church of St. Georghe. When they reached the pavement they split up, Woolcot walking away from Mason, towards the river, his contact taking the other direction. Mason's reaction was to duck again into the shadow of the colonnade of pillars until he reflected that this casually dressed Rumanian could not know him from any of the million or so inhabitants of the Jugoslavian capital.

He slipped unnoticed into the other's footsteps, following him round to the far side of the building, and saw him enter a rough parking lot situated behind the museum. With a hurried glance over his shoulder, the contact unlocked the door of what Mason thought at that distance looked like a new Lada, lit a cigarette and appeared to take something from the glove compartment. As he started to get out again, Mason turned quickly back towards Francuska Street, allowing the man to overtake him and continue as far as the south side of the museum, where he crossed the broad boulevard and disappeared into a building on the other side.

Mason waited for a few moments before following, keeping as his marker the doorway through which the man had entered. It was the entrance to the Café Kranj. Somewhere inside it he would have expected to find both the conspirators, but he continued walking, crossed the street lower down and then walked back, keeping a sharp eye on the Kranj. Since there was no further activity he found a bench opposite the restaurant, bought a local newspaper and used it for cover, musing to himself on the contents of the brown manilla envelope the contact had taken from the car. At a broad guess, the Rumanian had something for Woolcot to take back to London and there was a chance that Mason would catch the civil servant red-handed. At least he had satisfied himself on one point: Mike Woolcot was still up to something, but he would have to enter his cabin somehow to find out what that was.

Within minutes the Rumanian came outside, followed soon afterwards by Woolcot. They took opposite directions, the civil servant clutching his copy of the guide-book, from which there now protruded the brown manilla envelope. Feeling a little footsore from his wanderings across Belgrade, Mason rose gently from his seat and started to follow. A tram of three linked coaches trundled past on its way to the harbour, obstructing his view of the other pavement. Only when it had passed did he notice a familiar and startling sight. Mrs. Aveling was walking behind Woolcot at a distance of some thirty paces. Both were now headed towards the

Gallery of Fine Art, where there was an exhibition of Russian paintings.

Mason quickly crossed the street and tagged on behind, observing them eventually disappear inside the gallery. He would have followed them in immediately, but something held him back. Perhaps it was his awareness that Mrs. Aveling, accredited agent of the CIA, would know very well how to deal with the likes of Michael Woolcot. He himself might only get in the way.

While pacing up and down outside and glancing nervously at his watch, he noticed three figures suddenly approach the building from the opposite side of the street. At a shrewd guess they were not art fanciers. They had that measured gait, that immobility of expression that characterised the secret police. Mrs. Aveling had better watch her back, he mused, as he headed towards the tram stop. If Woolcot had really turned tables on her, she would need all the resources at her command. Had the young diplomat succeeded in leading the experienced and wily CIA agent into some kind of trap?

The automatic doors of his tram slammed shut as it began sliding down the long incline to the harbour. Suddenly behind him, peering all ways at once before crossing the road in the tram's wake, was remarkably the striking figure of Mrs. Walter B. Aveling! Mason lurched towards the rear tram window, lost his balance momentarily at the sudden roll of the vehicle and steadied himself to ascertain if it was really she. There could be no doubt about it. But where the heck was Mike Woolcot? He was surely the one who should have blithely emerged from the art gallery. Yet here was the American agent merging quickly with the crowd outside the Café Kranj. The detective turned and slumped heavily into a vacant seat, feeling frustrated, impotent and completely baffled. What on earth was really going on along this confounded river?

CHAPTER TWELVE

As George Mason stood against the ship's rail sipping a glass of lager to steady his nerves and listening with one ear to Clare's innocent chatter about the sights of Belgrade, there was an air of unreality; as if his holiday were over and he was now recalling it through partially shared experiences. From beyond the quay, the sinister world of espionage intruded, casting menacing shadows before it. Clare looked radiant beneath the shock of straw-blonde hair that she would dress before dinner, but which now fell freely to her tanned shoulders. She too was enjoying a drink, intent when not recounting her adventures on observing the bustle on the quay, the last-minute preparations before the boat put out for Budapest, the last port of call before Vienna.

"Didn't notice Mike slip aboard," she said, casting round in the hope of spotting him somewhere in the vicinity of the bar.

Mason did not reply. Not for the first time he felt really puzzled on her friend's account.

"Have you seen him, George?" she enquired. "Or are you still playing cat and mouse!"

"Here comes Magda, at least," he replied, pointing towards Dunavska Street, where the ample figure of the Intourist guide was fast approaching the dock. As she drew alongside she waved cheerily towards them. But there was still no sign of Mike Woolcot or of Anton Ziegler.

Magda's arrival on board was hailed by a sudden blast of the ship's siren echoing loud and clear round the small harbour. There followed the throbbing of the engines, shaking fitfully the whole framework of the ship. Mason glanced at his watch in apprehension.

Still there was no sign of the missing pair, as the ship's hands scrambled for the hawsers and the gangplank was raised. Still no shadow flit before the pink stucco; only the sunlit void of Dunavska Street.

"I'm going down to my cabin," Clare announced, "to change for dinner."

He thought it strange that she appeared unconcerned about Woolcot, and uneasy thoughts crossed his mind as to what exactly had taken place inside the austere walls of the Gallery of Fine Art. And what on earth had happened to Ziegler?

He burst in on the *Orsova* bridge, brushing aside Magda Semyonova's remonstrations.

"It is forbidden at this time to speak with the captain," she said, in her unidiomatic English. "All communication must be through Intourist. Please, Mr. Mason. The captain . . ."

Mason wrenched his arm free and confronted the captain vehemently. The latter merely glanced up from his task of steering the boat from the quay, prepared to overlook the intrusion, but not to be side-tracked from his job.

"I will speak with you later, Mr. Mason," he said. "As you can see, I am fully occupied."

"Captain, I must insist that you reverse the engines and return to the quay."

"Your friend has disappeared again?" the captain asked, drily.

"Two people from this party are missing!" Mason protested.

Magda stood beside him, in glowering incredulity.

"The *Orsova* must not sail until they turn up," Mason insisted, afraid that whatever material Woolcot had collected from his contact at the Kranj would go missing with him.

"Neither of them returned to the ship?" Magda asked, more sympathetically.

Mason shook his head.

"We cannot possibly upset the schedule," the captain said. "Unless you want to get me arrested. And your Mr. Woolcot is beginning to make a habit of this—most inconsiderate, Mr. Mason, wouldn't you say?"

Mason turned away as philosophically as he could with a glance towards the retreating sky-line of Belgrade. What the captain said was true enough. Woolcot had pulled something similar before, and turned up later with a ready explanation. He could hardly expect a river boat to upset its schedule, there were too many people involved, and currents and water levels to consider. And Mason saw no reason why he should worry over Ziegler, in view of the circumstances of Oliver's death. If he had run foul of the secret police, in his quest for antiquarian literature, let him stew in his own juice. There was no alternative now but to wait and see what happened in Budapest. But the curious feeling nagged at him that the American woman, Mrs. Aveling, should be the real object of his concern; yet there she was, an agent of the CIA, strolling about casually in broad daylight through the streets of Belgrade, having apparently eluded the secret police.

Clare Dyment relaxed in her cabin for a while, then took a shower in the cramped cubicle along the corridor to wash off the dust and the heat of the day's sightseeing. Before dressing for dinner she took her compact case, a fairly large rectangular one with her initials embossed on it, a present from a one-time admirer in London, opened it and slid her nail file behind the mirror. Satisfied that all was in order, she snapped the compact shut, completed her toilet and then went up to join George Mason for a dinner of poached salmon, not particularly concerned at this stage about Mike Woolcot's second failure to return to the ship.

"You still believe Mike is up to something, don't you?" she said, in answer to Mason's insinuations.

"The theories must fit the facts," the detective remarked, drily. "Woolcot and Ziegler may even be working in collusion. They have both made contact with the Ministry of Information in Bucharest. And now they are both missing in Belgrade. Ziegler's a cunning old fox, you can take my word for it."

"He didn't strike me as devious at all," Clare said, impatiently. "Rather a nice old gentleman. In fact, he reminds me of an uncle of mine; but he's dead now, poor dear."

So much for feminine intuition, Mason thought. Of everyone involved in this strange business Ziegler to his mind was the most ruthless, the most cunning, the most unscrupulous. But the girl, in the rose-haze world of the Danube cruise, its sunshine, its exotic food and enchanting folk music, was hardly disposed to place people in their true perspective. Seemingly innocent and carefree, it seemed natural to assume that other people were the same. Even Woolcot's second disappearance she appeared to take as something of a practical joke. Mason wanted to impress upon her the gravity of the situation.

"I am practically certain," he said, "that highly sensitive information is being carried to and from the United Kingdom by members of this cruise. Did you know that your Foreign Office friend has been in touch with a contact at least twice to my own knowledge?"

"In that case, what do you imagine he is doing still in Belgrade?"

Mason shrugged, refilled their wine glasses and said, half-seriously: "Perhaps he has defected."

Clare put down her wine just in time to avoid choking on it as she burst into laughter, causing the staid and respectable German passengers to turn their heads and stare.

"My word, George," she said humorously, "you do make the most preposterous claims! Even supposing Mike was guilty of these aberrations—which I incidentally think is absurd—the onus of proof would lie with you. He would know that you haven't a shred of tangible evidence. And why would he choose this particular time to defect?"

"Because he is aware of my suspicions," Mason said, undeterred. "He knows he will be finished once we get back to London."

Clare merely smiled. "I'll grant you one thing, George Mason," she said, tauntingly. "You're certainly good entertainment value. Never a dull moment when good old George is around."

Conversation was momentarily suspended while the waiter brought them dessert and coffee, in the impassive, impersonal way in which the crew were trained.

"I shall have evidence," Mason said, "given time."

The waiter was still there, at Mason's elbow, holding out a slim brown envelope. Mason took it, since it was obviously meant for him, and revolved it in his grasp.

"Go on," Clare urged, playfully, "open it. It may be a message from the KGB!"

"Do you think I dare?" he asked.

The girl was eagerly leaning forward, egging him on.

Mason slit down one edge with his table knife and slowly drew out a printed colour brochure.

"What do you make of it?" he said, passing it to her as soon as he had read it.

"A list of hotels," she replied, warily. "The sort of thing put out by tourist boards."

"Exactly right," he said. "Now read out the one underlined in red ink."

"Hotel Vlad, Budapest?" she began uncertainly, having difficulty with the strange name. "American breakfast, daily from 8.00 a.m."

Mason smiled quietly to himself, put the brochure back in its envelope and tucked it away in his inside jacket pocket.

"Any idea who it's from?" she asked, now quite serious.

"I could make a very good guess," he replied. "Why do you think someone would send me a list of officially approved hotels in Budapest? And underline one of them in particular?"

"Because they wanted you to go there, at a particular time."

"Precisely."

Something about him now aroused her sympathy. Her eyes had softened, the taunt had gone out of them, as if she now fully realised that he was up against something, out there in the hostile and unfamiliar world about them.

"That's enough of mysteries for one evening," he said, thinking that the sender of the envelope would have had plenty of time while the ship was berthed in Belgrade to slip on board and hand it, with instructions, to the waiter.

"Do you intend to go?" she asked, in obvious admiration.

"I'll decide that tomorrow," he replied. "On this cruise, almost anything can happen before then."

His eyes were now firmly on Clare and his thoughts on how they might spend the evening together. There was to be a disco in the forward lounge later on when dinner was over. He had brought her, he considered, to just the right pitch of sympathy and concern. The wine and the romantic atmosphere of the river would do the rest. And at night the river was at its most romantic, the outlines of ships slipping past in the darkness; the shadows on the shore; the lights, the stars, and the stillness of water.

CHAPTER THIRTEEN

M rs. Walter B. Aveling, her portable cassette recorder deep inside her shoulder bag, strolled along the embankment from the English Bridge, beneath the Romanesque ramparts of the Fishermen's Bastion rising sheer above the river and on towards Margaret Island. She enjoyed that aspect of Budapest, its associations with famous women; something which, together with her modest command of the language, gained over a period of several years, made her feel more at home here than in any other East European capital. She also had a high regard for its customs, traditions and artistic life, particularly for the music of Bartok and Kodaly, which was based on folk songs similar to those she spent her spare time collecting; and with which she would entertain the members of the Midwest Musicological Society in the course of her annual Fall Lecture.

It was with these cultural interests in mind that, having first ascertained from the Elizabeth Quay the precise time of arrival, allowing for tides and shallows, of the *Orsova*, she crossed the Margaret Bridge towards Pest, as far as the large island in midstream. Margaret Island was far more than an island in the Danube: it was the summer playground for the denizens of the city, whose cafés, parks and woodlands provided refreshment from the oppressive heat of the streets, the traffic fumes, and the hustle and bustle of modern life.

With about an hour to spare, she followed in the wake of the early strollers, rather thin on the ground at this hour of the day, as far as the Rose Garden. In the small restaurant there she ordered coffee with brandy and watched with keen interest the rehearsal for a matinee performance of the *csardas*, a peasant dance noted for its purity and grace. She instantly regretted not bringing along her portable camera; colour photographs of the costumes would have caused even greater heights of envy on the part of the lecture audience, who had generally to be content with what they could find in the pages of the National Geographic, to fill in the authentic detail.

Having deposited her cosmetics samples in a locker at the main railway station, she was free to manipulate her recording equipment, alternately sipping the strong aromatic coffee and the wine, and looking for all the world like the affluent American tourist she might easily have been taken for. Mrs. Aveling made no attempt to disguise either her nationality or her comparative wealth, in the knowledge that venues such as the Rose Garden were patronised only by tourists or higher party functionaries. She did not therefore feel conspicuous, but enjoyed the same savoir faire that she exhibited in the garden restaurant of the Hotel Florescu, Bucharest or in locating the dummy confessional in the Church of St. Georghe, whence she had observed both the dealings of Mr. Michael Woolcot and the clumsy attempts at eavesdropping on the part of George Mason.

And she had every right to feel at home. Her mandate from the Bliss Cosmetics Corporation, based in Detroit, provided her with a visa from the Hungarian Embassy in Washington, renewable annually, and the encouragement of the Hungarian authorities to introduce, to a limited degree, certain aspects of western consumer society that had a particular bearing on women. They reasoned, probably with justification, that a degree of official encouragement for such practices might suppress demands for the diversion of essential resources to the consumer field. And if the women were happy, the men would be more content. It was thus that Mrs. Walter B. Aveling had a fully approved and accredited role to play in the evolution of socialist societies; the blessing of the various socialist governments; of the Bliss Cosmetics Corporation; and the freedom and opportunity to indulge her favourite hobby, the collection of authentic folk music in a world full of artificiality and sham. Thus the performance of the *csardas* was to her almost akin to a religious experience.

Glancing round her, once the coveted music was safely encapsulated on tape, she now settled into a light morning snack of salt pancakes, with occasion once more to reflect upon the conservatism of socialist women in the matter of their physical appearance. Make-up, as people understood it and practised it in the West, that comprehensive battery of creams, sprays, pulvers, deodorants, rinses, mists and mascaras, was an unfamiliar quantity to the local population, who relied generally on the healthy, fresh complexion that was death to her own compatriots. It was a question of re-educating them, of getting at them young enough, at dance halls, hair salons, modelling schools; of placing *Vogue* or *Cosmopolitan* in strategic places, in waiting rooms, conveniences, cafés, on park benches. When she came to the point of sale, she relied on the simplest and most effective technique: her full colour range of Bliss lipsticks. It was thus that she hoped to introduce the womenfolk of the Communist world to the contemporary chic of their western counterparts, gain the Congressional Medal for Export and, if possible, the Lenin Peace Prize to boot.

The Rose Garden Restaurant grew noisy with the termination of the concert and the commencement of full breakfast service. The tables around her quickly filled with affluent German tourists, unmistakably from the *Orsova*, clamouring for table service. She lit a cigarette, checked her watch, an expensive Accutron bought by that darling idiot Everett in Bucharest, and surveyed these children of the economic miracle with slight disdain. She then paid her cheque and eased her spright, print-clad frame out of the garden chair. The *Orsova*, she calculated, would have berthed some time ago, allowing its passengers an easy stroll towards the Rose Garden. She would have to reach Belvaros, the inner city, by the most direct route possible, leaving the embankment by Roosevelt Square and picking her way carefully amid the maze of ancient streets to the Hotel Vlad. As she walked she appeared unaware that someone had picked up her trail.

George Mason had also risen early that morning, going straight up to the dining-room on A-deck for the usual light breakfast of coffee and rolls, amplified by a little cold meat. Moments after his arrival Clare Dyment, nautically clad in blue sweater and white slacks, came in, distracting him from his perusal of the hotel list handed to him in the brown envelope by the waiter at dinner.

"You seem in a great hurry this morning," she said, lightly.

"I woke up when we berthed," he said. "Must have been the sudden stopping of the ship's engines."

The Hotel Vlad, he now remembered, was the place he had first met the intriguing American lady, Mrs. Walter B. Aveling; and he imagined it had much more to offer on that particular summer morning than a lavish American breakfast.

"Aren't you worried about Mike?" he asked.

"He can take care of himself," came the quick response. "Probably show up just like last time, in the nick of time. But simply as a precaution I thought of going to the Embassy to see if they know anything."

"That will save me a job," Mason said, with satisfaction.

"Same old usual for breakfast?" she enquired, having never been particularly happy with coffee and rolls.

"With the addition of Magyar sausage," Mason replied. "Highly recommended. Or maybe, since it's to be the last morning of the cruise, you would prefer instead a full American breakfast"—he imagined the menu—"waffles in maple syrup, ham and egg grill, chilled fruit juices . . ."

"You must be kidding, George," she said. "Surely you're not going to go fishing round that crazy hotel. What was it called?"

"The Vlad."

"The very name gives me the creeps."

"That's not very surprising," he said, with an attempt at nonchalance. "It's named after Count Vlad, the original Dracula!"

"Then you really must be mad, George," she protested. "It's obvious someone's trying to set you up. And with Mike and old Ziegler already missing . . ."

"So you're not coming?" he said, in mock-disappointment.

Clare appeared to hesitate for a moment. Then she said: "Right now, I think I'd even enter Dracula's Castle for a real breakfast! And besides, who's going to take care of you?"

Mason's rather grim features broke into an affectionate smile, a smile which recalled the close intimacies of the previous evening, after the lights had gone out and the disco dancers had returned to their cabins on the lower decks. She obviously cared for him, but in a detached, flirting sort of way. She could give herself to him, yet remain the preserve of another. Not Mike Woolcot, since she betrayed no real personal concern at his absence. The American airman, perhaps? But it was irrelevant now. The holiday was almost over, and tonight they would reach Vienna. The safety, the security of the Austrian bank of the Danube had for him at that moment a great appeal.

"If you don't mind," she said, "I'll just have some coffee now. Then we'll go."

"But I must make just one proviso," he said, cautiously.

"Oh? And what is that?"

"You must make your own way there." To quench her obvious alarm, he added: "Don't worry, I'll draw you a map. In any case you can't miss it. Right opposite the cathedral; a charming, old-world sort of place."

"I suppose you have good reasons," she said, puzzled and a little disappointed.

"Just a precaution," he reassured her. "In case we're followed. When you reach the hotel wait a few minutes and then order. Don't worry if I am a little late. I'll be there."

Clare sipped her coffee, nibbled at one of the rolls, then returned to her cabin to collect her purse before leaving the ship. Why had he invited her to the Vlad, he wondered, as her footsteps died out along the deck? Perhaps because he felt in need of a witness who could corroborate his version of events. But more likely because the presence of a girl, a young and attractive girl who seemed to have no connection with the bizarre events taking place around him, might provide him with some kind of shield. But from what? The only person he could associate with the Hotel Vlad was the CIA agent, Mrs. Aveling.

Five minutes later he went out onto the deck, just to check that she had set off in the right direction, but Clare had already disappeared from sight amid the tall waterfront buildings. He watched instead as the sightseeing bus drew up alongside the boat, with all the familiarity of routine; except that this could be no ordinary morning in Budapest. It was a day when something was going to happen; when something had to happen to snap the taut wires of tension built up over the last few days, ever since Oliver Markham's strange and sinister death in the Black Sea, hundreds of river miles behind them; and the sudden disappearance of Woolcot and Ziegler.

When he finally left the ship he took a circuitous route to the hotel through the maze of narrow streets winding through the old city. But he had not foreseen the complexity and similarity of many of these alleys, which wound back into themselves without advancing his objective. He felt lost when he reached Petofi Street for the third time and recognised the same pastry shop with the blind half-lowered. Or was it a different shop? There were many such shops in old Budapest. He grew fearful and anxious about his appointment, sensing now that he would be very late, that the girl would fret.

It was then that he noticed, keeping abreast of him on the opposite pavement, a figure that looked vaguely familiar. He was being watched and shadowed! With mounting panic he continued along Petofi Street, wondering with vague helplessness if he could not shake his pursuer off. When the man quickened his gait and crossed the street behind him, he recognised at once the Rumanian whom Mike Woolcot had met in Bucharest and Belgrade. Incredibly, he had turned up here too, in the heart of Budapest. Had Woolcot sent him to do his dirty work for him amid these quiet, cloistered streets? Or was he there to act as a kind of goad, to make sure that Mason duly arrived at the Hotel Vlad, where the final scene in the drama was about to unfold before the assembled conspirators. All in it together, perhaps even the ingenuous Clare Dyment, just waiting to humiliate and defeat George Mason. It might have appeared very much that way to him, as the Rumanian rapidly overtook him and led him to within a stone's throw of the hotel entrance, before somehow melting from sight in the crowded cathedral square.

Mason paused for breath at the hotel steps, then resolutely entered, crossed the wide foyer and stepped into the restaurant, his senses jolted by the mingled aromas of maple syrup and ham and eggs. Clare Dyment was sitting over by the far wall already eating her breakfast. She glanced up as if to warn him, but Mason's attention had already become riveted, in the automaton way in which he now moved, by a second presence deeper into the restaurant, but partially hidden by a bamboo screen. In her full regalia of broad-brimmed hat and print dress sat Mrs. Walter B.

Aveling, observing every step of his approach through tinted spectacles. She too appeared to be eating an American breakfast and she was alone. Curiously, since Mason had half expected them, there was no sign of Woolcot or Ziegler, and the awareness inspired a momentary optimism. Mrs. Aveling put down her knife and fork, smiled candidly towards him and said:

"Charming of you to drop in, Inspector Mason."

Even as she spoke and gave her cosmetic smile of welcome, he was aware of a third presence which had at first been completely hidden by the bamboo screen. Across the parquet floor fell the shadow of a gun. The realisation roused him from his stupor. His mind worked with lightning precision and speed. In the crowded restaurant they would not dare risk a shot. He could still turn and dash back through the crowded restaurant, overpower the Rumanian in the street and escape amid the teeming alleys of the Belvaros. But even as he rehearsed this move in his mind he felt a sharp prod between his shoulder blades and found himself propelled towards the bamboo screen. Escape was now impossible.

"You surely did not imagine, Inspector Mason," Mrs. Aveling said, "that we could allow you to return to Vienna until you have told us what you know of the book conspiracy. Mr. Ferenc here, of the State Police, has made arrangements for your stay in Budapest." Ferenc emerged from behind the screen, grimacing with menace, while the third party moved to cover him from the front. They knew nothing, was Mason's reaction, despite the determined efforts of Mrs. Aveling.

"I should have thought Woolcot or Ziegler would have told you all you wish to know. Didn't you have them both arrested at the Gallery of Fine Art in Belgrade?"

"Very observant of you, Mr. Mason," the American said.

"Of course Herr Ziegler was as interested in the book as we are, but I am afraid equally as unsuccessful in locating its more interesting contents."

"How do you know he was telling you the truth?"

"We made quite certain of that."

"And Mike Woolcot?"

"To our certain knowledge, he has been in contact with saboteurs of the peoples' socialist republics. He will be put on trial."

"The brown package he received in Belgrade?"

"Material of considerable value to NATO," Mrs. Aveling said, "that had been carefully collected for him along the way. Perhaps you were unaware that Mr. Woolcot was combining business with pleasure?"

Mason made no reply, not wishing to say anything to further incriminate Woolcot, and kicking himself now for being so wrong about him. He should have paid more attention to Clare.

"That brings us down to you, Mr. Mason," she said, matter-of-factly, "by process of elimination. Woolcot's copy of the guidebook contained—at least when it left London it contained—a piece of information of the utmost importance to my superiors."

"Which ones?" asked Mason drily.

Mrs. Aveling ignored the jibe. Consuming the rest of the waffles unhurriedly, she said: "Mr. Ferenc and I are confident you can help us locate it. He has a residence available in the southern outskirts of the city. He will take you there now and report back to me over lunch in this hotel. Take my advice, Mr. Mason, and be co-operative. These people are experts."

"My car is waiting for you," Ferenc said, as the man with the gun motioned him forward. "At the rear of the hotel."

"But . . ." Mason said, half turning towards Clare's table.

"Your friend Miss Dyment will be unharmed. She will be free to return to the ship."

At the rear of the hotel, a black official-looking sedan drove up silently over the smooth cobbles and jerked to a halt. The nearside rear door opened and Ferenc bundled Mason inside, stooping then to the driver's window to give hurried instructions. The sedan then sped off recklessly through the narrow streets towards the outskirts of Budapest. As they crossed the Margaret Bridge, Mason glimpsed the cold black water beneath them, the swirling currents and the large commercial barges ferrying coal down-river. It was only when they were well clear of the city and approaching the woods to the south that his anxiety gave way to muted optimism. There was something very familiar about the driver, who was screened from him by the glass partition. Take away the dark-green uniform and cap and it looked very much like Woolcot's Rumanian contact, the man he had earlier noticed walking ahead of him, as if leading him, through the Belvaros; the difference now being, of course, following Mrs. Aveling's disclosures, that he could regard him as a friend. But how on earth had he got into the front seat of the car, and who had tipped him off about the likely sequence of events at the Hotel Vlad? Mason tried desperately to make himself heard, but there was no response as the large sedan left the highway and continued for some distance along the forest track before suddenly swerving to a halt in a small clearing. The driver jumped out, opened the rear door for Mason to scramble out, then ran to unlock the boot. Inside was the gagged and trussed figure of the official driver of the car, whom the Rumanian now cut free.

"Is that really wise?" Mason asked, recovering from his surprise.

The Rumanian smiled. "He won't dare show his face in Budapest for a long time. You can be sure of that!"

"You have been trailing me all the time, since I left the *Orsova*," Mason said, non-plussed.

"You can thank your friend, Mr. Woolcot, for that," the other replied. "He thought you might need some assistance when things began to hot up."

"But how . . . ?"

"Explanations later, Mr. Mason. We have to get you across the border by nightfall. You may not now safely return to the boat."

"What about Clare Dyment?"

"You shall meet her briefly at the British Embassy. From there she will return to the cruise, unsuspected and unharmed, and arrive as scheduled in Vienna tomorrow evening."

"But how do I get out? Not in this thing!" he said, derisorily indicating the car. "We'll be arrested inside two hours."

"Everything has been carefully arranged for you in advance, Mr. Mason. Please to remain calm and leave everything in our hands. By the way, my name is Nicolae. You may call me Nick."

By the time Mason arrived at the Embassy, he was in a mood for explanations. Nicolae left the black sedan in an underground car park and led him on foot through a maze of back streets to the rear entrance of the building, where they were met by the First Secretary, Andrew Forshaw.

"You let me walk right into that," he said, "back there at the hotel. I might have been . . ."

"Shot, Mr. Mason? It was a calculated risk," Forshaw said. "And since you had evidently been expressing close interest in this case, we thought we could count on your co-operation."

"You thought you could set me up like a sitting duck," Mason said. "You might at least have kept me in the picture."

"That," came the reply, "was the hardest decision of all. But as things turned out, you played your part very well. Your unmasking of Mrs. Aveling was superb. We had our suspicions, but not until this morning could we be sure that she was acting as a double agent. The incident at the hotel proved that conclusively."

"Where is Clare?" Mason asked, with concern.

"On her way here, I imagine." He glanced uncertainly towards the Rumanian, who nodded.

"Is that wise, in the circumstances?"

"Who would suspect her?" the Secretary asked.

"Then what about Mike Woolcot? All along I had him marked as the traitor."

"Only because he was carrying with him the key edition of *Bannerman's Guide*. It was loaned him by an American airman, based in London."

"And it contained information of value to the Comecon powers?" Mason proffered.

"Unfortunately for us, Mr. Mason, Woolcot never knew of the existence of that information. Whatever it was, it went missing at some point along the river. Our only conclusion must be that it somehow found its way into the hands of those it was originally intended for, presumably the Russians."

"That book never left the hands of the British party," Mason said, adamantly. "Not until old Ziegler managed to get hold of it in Mammaia. And I have it on very good authority that even he drew a blank."

"Ah, yes, Herr Ziegler," Forshaw said. "We could never really understand why the *Siegfried* people were so interested. Their sole interest is the security of former Nazis."

Something flashed through Mason's mind, but it had nothing to do with *Siegfried*. It was astonishingly simple, but at the same time profoundly disturbing. Yet there were very good reasons why it had not occurred to him before. Who would have suspected a woman?

At that point Clare entered the room. Glancing round for barely a moment, she rushed into Mason's arms. "Thank God you're safe, George," she exclaimed, clasping him tightly to her. "I've been so worried for you ever since you left the hotel."

"You might have had good cause," Mason said philosophically, holding her slightly away from him so that he could look her squarely in the face, to see if she was holding anything back.

"Are you sure you were not followed?" Forshaw asked, breaking into what was beginning to seem like a private party.

Clare shook her head vigorously.

"No, I made sure of that. The police boarded the tram three stops back and began to check papers. I almost had kittens. But they were looking for a man, I think. They ignored the women passengers. All five of us."

"All you have to do now, Miss Dyment," Forshaw said, "now that you have satisfied yourself about the safety of Mr. Mason— she wouldn't leave Budapest without that assurance, George—is to keep a cool head, return to the boat and resume your cruise to Vienna, as if nothing had happened. Report to Major Peter Lang on arrival in London."

"To Chief Inspector Harrington," Mason said, quickly. "He'll put you on to the Major."

"What about Mike?" Clare asked, with evident concern.

Everyone looked downcast at the mention of his name.

"He was betrayed to the secret police by Mrs. Aveling," Nicolae explained. "They trapped him at the Art Gallery in Belgrade. Unfortunately for him he was carrying a small package I had given him at the Café Kranj only minutes earlier. I'm afraid . . ."

". . . he'll be put on trial?" Mason asked.

Nicolae slowly nodded, as they all became aware of what that would mean.

"What are his chances of release?" Clare asked, eventually.

"In a case like this," Forshaw said, "a lot depends on the view the authorities choose to take. The material given him by our friend here would certainly be sufficient to convict him. But, as so often happens in such cases, he may be used as a pawn in a possible exchange. We'll have to work on that angle as much as we can without holding out too much hope."

"And what about you, George?" Clare asked. "The Hungarian police are sure to be looking out for you."

"Nicolae has made all the arrangements necessary to get Inspector Mason across the Austrian border. You can rest assured, Miss Dyment, that he will be waiting for you in Vienna when your ship docks. It's only a few hours drive from here, and Nicolae knows the perfect place to cross."

"In that case, George," Clare said, on leaving, "see you in Vienna. Gosh, to think I'll be the only one of the five of us who set out to complete the round trip on the *Orsova*."

"Six, if Herr Ziegler re-appears," Mason said. To him, this sudden turn in events had all the excitement and flavour of a resistance escape in the last war, the sort of thing he had only read about in books. It seemed an odd way to be ending a Danube cruise in the nineteen eighties, and he anticipated a deal of leg-pulling by Harrington when—if—he got safely back.

"I shall miss you for dinner, George," she said, on her way out.

CHAPTER FOURTEEN

George Mason spent most of the next morning catching up on the sights of Vienna he had missed in his scramble from train to boat two weeks ago. Two weeks! It seemed as many months, so eventful had his intended rest-cure turned out to be. And even now, he had the strong suspicion that although he had put the Danube River behind him, the beautiful, majestic, awe-inspiring Danube, seen the death of Oliver Markham and the abrupt departure of Gayle Sumner, the arrest of Mike Woolcot and Anton Ziegler, witnessed the treachery of Mrs. Walter B. Aveling, barely escaped with his own life, the ghost of the river was still not laid. There was one more link to fit into place, to complete the bizarre sequence of events.

He was in good time at the Danube Quay to watch the stately approach of the *Orsova*, holding to the left-hand bank past the large amusement park and the giant Ferris wheel. As it drew closer he could clearly make out the radiant, sun-tanned features of Clare Dyment, gazing out with all the ingenuousness of the young, captivated traveller at the approaching sky-line of Vienna. The moment she caught sight of him she waved fitfully to catch his attention. But there was no need: his watery eyes had picked her out long ago, amid the stolid ranks of the German passengers lining the ship's rail. Within half an hour, passengers and luggage were unloaded onto the quay.

"You made it, George," she said, running up to him. "I've been so worried about you all the way from Budapest."

"It's you who deserves the medal," he said, "for being the only one to complete the cruise."

She turned and glanced wistfully at the ship.

"You know," she said, "in spite of everything, I'm really sorry it's all over."

"An experience of a life-time?"

"I know I'll never do it again. I never could go that way again, after all that's happened."

"But it's still something you'd like to remember for the rest of your life?"

"I wouldn't have missed it for the world."

They took a taxi from the quayside, through what seemed the far friendlier, the far more hospitable streets of Vienna, the unmistakable ambiance and affluence of the West, the crossroads between East and West Europe.

"How did you get so easily across the border?" she wanted to know, as soon as they were comfortably seated in the train to Munich.

"It was like an escape operation from the war," Mason said. "Woolcot's friend, Nicolae, drove me through the night by car to the outskirts of the last town inside the Hungarian border. We stopped at a farm around 5 a.m. this morning. One of the farm trucks regularly makes a run with produce to the small towns on the Austrian side. The guard at the checkpoint was half-asleep. He may have checked papers, but I don't think so. We stopped less than half a minute. A routine run, Nicolae explained. They do it every day. But as you see," he remarked, fingering his beard, "I haven't had the opportunity to shave."

"Poor old George," Clare said, sympathetically, "riding through the small hours in a cattle truck."

"Well, a vegetable truck at least," he said, diffidently.

"And all on account of a..."

"Of a what, Clare?" he asked quickly.

She floundered for a moment, but quickly pulled herself together.

"I don't know," she said. "Whatever it was everyone was looking for back there."

"Have you any idea what that was?" he asked, pointedly.

Clare did not look him straight in the eye, as she replied: "Would I have let you all keep up that wild goose chase if I had?"

"It depends," he said, with an ingenuous smile, "on whatever it was we were all after."

Clare froze that line of enquiry with a fixed look through the carriage window, as the Munich train picked up speed through the Viennese oberland.

"Whatever it was," he said, genially, "I expect it found its way into the hands of the person or persons it was destined for."

"I expect so, too, George," she said, giving him a queer, guarded look. "Frankly, I've had enough of mysteries. I just want to go home and have a rest. Then get back to work as usual. Gosh, work seems a lifetime ago."

"I know the feeling," he said, visualizing his next meeting with Harrington.

"And what about Mike?" he asked.

She gave a sad, wistful smile.

"That's the one thing I really regret about this whole damn business," she said. "Why he had to go getting himself involved with secret agents and suchlike when he was supposed to be on a holiday, I'll never understand."

"Perhaps he was under instructions," Mason suggested. "Must have been a big deal—high priority."

"I expect he was," she said. "In our job, the right hand never knows what the left is doing. It's often the way things are."

"And you never know which side anyone is on. I mean really deep inside people."

"I suppose you don't," she said, with a nervous little laugh.

"Look at Philby and Burgess and Maclean."

"I know," she replied. "The occupant of the next desk can be a traitor."

"I think I'll stick to my own job," he said, with a shudder that was caused by the train suddenly entering a windy tunnel.

"That might be very wise," she said, with a nervous smile.

Some twenty hours later, following a fitful ride in the overnight sleeper from Munich to Ostend, and a reviving breakfast on the cross-channel ferry, a full English breakfast, George Mason and Clare Dyment arrived rather travel-weary at Waterloo Station.

"I suppose this is where we say good-bye," Clare said, heading for the barrier to the Bakerloo Line after tactfully resisting Mason's offer to see her home and help with her luggage. "Haven't you forgotten something?" he asked.

Clare turned at the last minute and glanced at him, quite tensely he thought, since they were only saying farewell.

"Your telephone number," he said, smiling disarmingly.

Clare was already through the ticket barrier. She shouted back her number, gave a little friendly wave, picked up her two suitcases and disappeared down the escalator.

Mason watched until she was out of sight. Time was on his side for the next couple of hours or so. She would return home to rest up for a while after the tiring journey. Then, if his calculations were correct, she would go out again in the early evening. He wanted to make sure he could check her first social call on her return from the Danube cruise. In his view, that would be the most significant call she would make. He had already, for various reasons, crossed off Gayle Sumner from his list of suspects, from the list of those cruise members who had early access to Mike Woolcot's book. Gayle Sumner, he knew, was not one of them. She had relied too heavily on Oliver Markham; on poor unfortunate Oliver, for whom the *Orsova* cruise had turned out so tragically.

Unhurriedly, he picked up his single large suitcase and headed for the bank of telephone booths opposite the buffet on the mainline station. As he reached inside his jacket pocket for loose change to make the call, his hand came against something hard and metallic. In an instant he knew that was something he had meant to give Clare before their parting: the compact case which had fallen out of her loosely-secured shoulder bag as they came through customs at Dover. He had been several paces behind her, and he remembered now slipping it into his side pocket so that he could reach for his passport.

"The devil!" he thought, since that would mean an open contact with her when he wanted to cover her movements as quietly and inconspicuously as possible. Taking out the offending object, he revolved it slowly in his hand, wondering how best to approach her with it. Should he take it straight away, or wait until tomorrow and tell her he had overlooked it? She would soon discover its loss, if she hadn't done so already, and would be grateful for its return. As he toyed with it, the catch slipped and the compact fell open in his grasp. Holding it at arm's length, he surveyed with concern the two days' growth of stubble across his chin and rubbed his free hand against it before noticing that something appeared to be protruding slightly along one edge of the compact mirror. He moved his thumb against it, and it bent easily under the pressure. With the thumb and index-finger of his free hand, his pulse quickening in excitement, he drew out an old black-and-white photograph, held it in the light and knit his brows in puzzlement. The light of understanding soon dawned across his travel-strained features as he recalled the subject of his conversation with the embassy First Secretary in Belgrade. He now had in his possession the object of Herr Ziegler's compulsive interest in *Bannerman's Guide*, and the apparent reason for his murder of Oliver Markham: a picture of a group of S.S. officers taken during the war. Clare must have removed it from Woolcot's book quite early on, and the thought which now crossed Mason's mind was whether she had realised its full significance. But if not, he reasoned, why had she not shown it to him on the cruise?

Carefully, he placed the photograph inside his wallet, took out a ten-pence coin, entered one of the telephone booths and dialled Directory Enquiries to obtain the full postal address of the Kensington telephone number Clare had given him only minutes ago. She would not only be upset, he thought, at losing her compact; she would be extremely concerned. Now there would be no time at all to lose to check her movements once she had safely deposited her luggage at her home address.

CHAPTER FIFTEEN

At precisely 7.29 that evening, Clare Dyment rang the doorbell of 31 Launceston Gardens, Belgravia. The door was opened by a maid who, instantly recognising her, showed her into the drawing-room at the end of the short, panelled hall; a room filled with expensive antique furniture and several original works of art. Sinking back into the plush upholstery, she caught her breath after a hurried walk from the tube station, still racking her brain, as she had done for the last few hours, over where she could have placed her compact case.

"Clare, darling," a voice said, when the drawing-room door opened again. "Wonderful to see you back. Had a good trip?"

The girl did not rise, but held her arms out while the man stooped to embrace her. He was a man considerably older than Clare Dyment, a man whose mode of dress and general bearing spoke of high rank in the Civil Service.

"Edward, it was simply wonderful!" she said, drawing him onto the sofa beside her. "I never imagined a river cruise could be so fascinating, so varied, so full of interest."

"And you look terrific," Edward said, in admiration. "Obviously it's done you a lot of good."

"Food wasn't bad—better than I expected, in fact. Weather was terrific: and, of course, things happened."

"Over the phone earlier," Edward said, solicitously, "you sounded worried."

Clare coloured slightly in her embarrassment.

"On the journey back from Vienna I did something very foolish."

Edward's brow puckered.

"You fell in love?" he asked, apprehensively.

The girl almost burst into laughter at the anxiety in her lover's face, but the matter was far too serious for that.

"I lost my compact," she said, seizing her psychological advantage to make a clean breast of it.

"The one I gave you last Christmas?"

She nodded tearfully.

"If that is all," he said, "I'll buy you a new one."

Clare leaned over and kissed him on the cheek.

"That's very sweet of you, Edward, but I don't really think you are going to be quite so forgiving."

"You just try me and see," he replied.

Clare took a deep breath.

"I told you a moment ago," she said, "that things happened on the ship."

"What sort of things? Did the crew defect in Vienna? Did Mike propose to you?"

"Now you're not taking me seriously," she complained.

"Go on then, seriously. No more jokes."

"It was the strangest experience in some ways," she began. "You see, a number of very different people seemed interested in the same book, in *Bannerman's Guide*."

"Like the one you took with you?"

"Exactly, except that for some reason it was Mike's copy they were all interested in."

"*Who*, Clare? Be precise."

"There was this American woman first, then a Swiss book dealer called Ziegler. Then a Rumanian snatched my book from a church porch in Belgrade."

"Go on," he said, growing more attentive by the minute.

"I happened to be the first person on board to whom Mike lent his copy of the book. We exchanged copies in fact, just to compare them."

"So?" he said, rising from the sofa to pour them both a drink.

"While I was glancing through it, I accidentally dropped the book on the ship's deck. It fell quite hard and dislodged something that had been concealed in the spine. When I picked it up again, I noticed a rolled-up photograph protruding slightly at one side.

Lucky I was on my own at the time. George Mason had just gone to get the drinks."

"George Mason?"

"Believe it or not, a police inspector on holiday from the Special Branch! And he soon started asking questions, hatching theories and raising suspicions."

"Good God!" Edward said, his face growing several shades paler. "You knew that Cramer loaned Woolcot that book?"

"That's what I thought," Clare said. "And I knew you had close contact with Cramer. I couldn't be sure if Mike was aware of the photograph and, if so, of what it might signify."

"So you kept it to yourself in case somebody else discovered it? Bright girl, Clare."

Clare smiled, and appeared to relax a little.

"In fact, Mike knew nothing about the photograph. I found that much out by indirect questioning."

"So you still kept it concealed?"

"By that time it was obvious that practically the whole boat was speculating on what the guidebook might contain. George Mason, for one, was as keen as mustard. Snatching guidebooks became the *leitmotif* of the entire voyage!"

Edward's face broke into a huge smile.

"So Clare had the goods from the start. Excellent! Except that it was supposed to be picked up by a KGB agent somewhere along the way. Cramer was arranging all that through the American network."

"Mrs. Aveling!" Clare said at once, remembering the interlude at the Vlad Hotel. "She was a double agent. Not a very good one, I'm afraid. She never did get hold of Mike's copy."

"Then thank heavens you got to it first. Otherwise all our heads would roll."

"Is it that important?" Clare asked, nervously.

"It's blackmail evidence against the senior officer of MI5 who's been detailed to investigate Cramer. Man by the name of Lang. Major Peter Lang."

It was Clare's turn to grow pale. Everyone had heard of Lang.

"That photograph should have been lodged in the files of the KGB, to keep Lang off our necks. It shows him as an officer in the S.S.—something he'd prefer to keep a very close secret."

"But it isn't," Clare said, bursting into tears. "I concealed the photograph behind the mirror of my compact case!"

Edward got up and paced the room agitatedly, deep furrows of concentration appearing in his brow. It was several minutes before he spoke. "Then you must find it," he snapped. "At all costs, find it!"

"I can't," she said. "I've searched everywhere, time and time again."

"If it's lost, it's lost," Edward said, more reasonably. "No one who found it would attribute the least significance to it. So long as Lang never finds that out, we're O.K. It has served its purpose."

"It's good of you to see it that way," Clare said, with the beginnings of a smile. "I've been feeling such a fool."

"Come on," he said. "Cheer up. We'll go through to dinner, and after that we'll talk some more."

"Well, well!" said Chief Inspector Harrington, when George Mason turned up at his office first thing the following morning. "Look what the tide brought in!"

Mason's eyebrows raised perceptibly: the man hadn't lost his bite in Mason's absence.

"Had a good trip?"

"Excellent," Mason said, his eyes warming at the memory.

"But not very relaxing, I gather. Frankly, Mason, you look washed out. And I gave you express orders to have a rest."

Mason smiled ironically and parked himself in the swivel chair facing Harrington's desk. His tiredness was easily explained by his rough journey out of Hungary and the stint of unexpected overtime he had been forced to put in last evening tailing Clare Dyment.

"And what have you brought me back? A whole bevy of secret agents, if your telegrams were anything to go by."

"Two of them ended up in custody in Belgrade," Mason said. "Mike Woolcot, of the Foreign Office, who apparently was legitimate all along. And Anton Ziegler, the *Siegfried* agent."

"I've been wondering about him," Harrington said. "Did you manage to find out the reason for his interest in the book?"

"I hope this is going to mean a lot more to you than it does to me," his colleague replied, removing the photograph from his wallet and passing it across the desk. If it doesn't, then we lose out."

"Is this what they were all after?" Harrington asked, eyeing it sceptically.

Mason nodded. "There was a girl friend of Mike Woolcot's on board the ship, Clare Dyment."

"I remember you asked me to check her out."

"She must have removed this from the book quite early on, and kept us all guessing."

"A group of Nazi officers," Harrington remarked. "Now wait a minute," he went on. "The chap in the middle looks vaguely familiar." He passed it back to his colleague.

"Means nothing to me."

"This *Siegfried* outfit," Harrington explained, "apparently exists to protect ex-Nazis, find employment for them, cover-up identities, and so on."

"So Ziegler's interest would be to prevent this photograph falling into the wrong hands, presumably to protect some highly-placed former Nazi from exposure, arrest and possible prosecution."

"Exactly," Harrington said. "There was even a tip-off some time ago, regarding a member of MI5."

"But not named?"

"Of course not. Hand me back that picture."

Harrington took it towards the window and held it in the light. After a few moments he commenced the sort of off-key whistling which generally indicated to Mason that his chief was on to something.

"Could be wrong," Harrington said, "since this is quite an old photograph. But I think I've met this gentleman before. The high cheek bones and the intensity of the eyes suggest a certain Major— but I couldn't possibly be right."

"Major who?" Mason asked, impatiently.

"It just *could* be," Harrington said, excitedly. "There's been an investigation going on at the American Embassy concerning that airman fellow, Cramer. Suspicion of gaining access to confidential papers, and involvement in a London-based spy ring. We've known of the existence of such a ring for some time, and it's supposed to penetrate into public life. But so far, no evidence."

"Cramer was the one who loaned Woolcot the book in the first place," Mason said, rising to his feet. "With that photograph in it!"

A slow smile spread across the heavy features of the senior detective. "Major Peter Lang has consistently reported no progress in the case."

"Do you think this is Lang?" Mason said, in disbelief.

"I'm not saying it is Lang," Harrington corrected. "I'm saying I think it could be him."

"How will you find out?"

"Face him with it. Tell him we know everything and accuse him outright. If we're right, he'll have kittens on the spot, or my name's not Bill Harrington. If we're wrong, he'll just laugh us in the face: it'll be so preposterous."

"What you are implying is that this photograph was being used as blackmail evidence against him, to stay his hand in official investigations?"

"Why else," asked Harrington, "would Cramer send it on a one-way ticket down the Danube?"

Mason resumed his seat and smiled in keen satisfaction. All that footwork and sweating it out through the capitals of Eastern Europe, his near liquidation at the hands of the Hungarian Secret Police, were not to be wasted after all.

"You did extremely well to come by this information, Mason," Harrington said warmly. "I'm going to see that you get a special commendation for it."

If Harrington could only guess the half of what he'd been through, Mason thought, to earn those rare words of praise.

"If we're right about Lang," Harrington said, "that leaves us one big job to do to clear up all this little business hinging on Lieutenant Cramer. We'll shop the whole hornets' nest of them."

"Oh?" said Mason guardedly, "and what is that?"

"We've got to find the identity of S. He's right at the top of the tree, with an official position in Whitehall. Now we don't want him retiring in a few years' time on an index-linked public service pension, do we Inspector Mason?"

"No, sir," Mason replied, dutifully. "We do not."

"I don't suppose your recent researches," Harrington said hopefully, "give us any pointers in that direction?"

"Who do we know, Chief Inspector," Mason said, with a sly smile, "residing at 31 Launceston Gardens, Belgravia?"

Harrington quickly consulted his filing cabinet.
"Not Sir Edward Hamer!" he said, with an incredulous gasp.
"And who might he be?"
"Permanent Under-Secretary at the Air Ministry," Harrington said, almost in ecstasy. "Go on, Mason, I'll buy it. Tell me everything."

Printed in the United States
59681LVS00002B/56

9 781413 487527